MW00929960

THE GRIMSBANE FAMILY WITCH HUNTERS

THE
GRIMSBANE FAMILY
WITCH HUNTERS

JOAN REARDON

ALADDIN

NEW YORK LONDON TORONTO SYDNEY NEW DELHI

ALADDIN

An imprint of Simon & Schuster Children's Publishing Division
1230 Avenue of the Americas, New York, New York 10020
First Aladdin hardcover edition August 2024
Text copyright © 2024 by Joan Reardon
Jacket illustrations copyright © 2024 by Jamie Green
All rights reserved, including the right of reproduction in whole or in part in any form.
ALADDIN and related logo are registered trademarks of Simon & Schuster, LLC.
Simon & Schuster: Celebrating 100 Years of Publishing in 2024
For information about special discounts for bulk purchases, please contact
Simon & Schuster Special Sales at 1-866-506-1949 or business@simonandschuster.com.
The Simon & Schuster Speakers Bureau can bring authors to your live event. For more
information or to book an event, contact the Simon & Schuster Speakers Bureau
at 1-866-248-3049 or visit our website at www.simonspeakers.com.
Designed by Heather Palisi
The text of this book was set in Warnock Pro.
Manufactured in the United States of America 0724 BVG
2 4 6 8 10 9 7 5 3 1
Library of Congress Cataloging-in-Publication Data
Names: Reardon, Joan, author.
Title: The Grimsbane family witch hunters / Joan Reardon.
Description: First Aladdin hardcover edition. | New York : Aladdin, 2024. |
Audience: Ages 8 to 12. | Summary: "Twelve-year-old Anna Grimsbane journeys into
monster-filled woods to save her brother, who has been cursed by a witch known as
the Watcher"—Provided by publisher.
Identifiers: LCCN 2023053095 (print) | LCCN 2023053096 (ebook) |
ISBN 9781665929561 (hardcover) | ISBN 9781665929585 (ebook)
Subjects: CYAC: Twins—Fiction. | Siblings—Fiction. | Blessing and cursing—Fiction. |
Forests and forestry—Fiction. | Witches—Fiction. | Monsters—Fiction. |
LCGFT: Paranormal fiction. | Novels.
Classification: LCC PZ7.1.R3973 Gr 2024 (print) | LCC PZ7.1.R3973 (ebook) |
DDC [Fic]—dc23
LC record available at https://lccn.loc.gov/2023053095
LC ebook record available at https://lccn.loc.gov/2023053096

To my parents, for the hours you spent reading to me;
to Shannon and Timmy, for always having my back;
and to Ben, for being my everything

Table of Contents

THE GRIMSBANE FAMILY WITCH HUNTERS

1

A Grim Family Business

Anna Grimsbane's twin brother, Billy, was growing up too fast, and Anna wasn't growing up fast enough. In just one week, they were going to turn thirteen. For most kids, this was an exciting day marked with balloons and birthday cake and a peaceful transition into teenagehood. Unfortunately, the second midnight struck on the Grimsbane twins' birthday, their life as they knew it would be over. Basic activities would turn dangerous for Billy. For him, something as simple as stepping on a skateboard would become akin to skydiving during a lightning storm—an easy way to guarantee his untimely, unusual, and unpleasant death. Anna couldn't even do anything about it—not yet, anyway.

This problem was at the forefront of Anna's mind as she skateboarded home on a chilly, gray afternoon, much like all afternoons in Witchless, Indiana—"the Cryptid Capital of the USA." Anna zoomed down the sidewalk, passing colonial storefronts bedecked with dramatic displays featuring pumpkins, acorns, witches, and ghosts. She bobbed and weaved through the crowd of monster-obsessed tourists who swarmed Witchless every autumn in hopes of spotting Bigfoot, the Mothman, or even a jackalope lurking in the dense forest surrounding the town. The wind whipped at Anna's long black hair and popped with a magical energy that hinted that Halloween was just around the corner.

Anna shifted the drink carrier full of coffee in her right hand, making sure not to spill the bag of scones in her left. She sped through a pile of leaves and sent them scattering like confetti in her wake.

An elderly couple exchanged a pained look as Anna rocketed past, shaking their heads.

"Just as strange as the others," the old woman muttered.

The old man nodded in agreement.

Most people in Witchless found Anna's family odd, though they typically turned a blind eye toward the

Grimsbanes' behavior—either because they actually believed the stories about cryptids lurking in the Not-So-Witchless Woods, or because they appreciated the economic boom that came with tourism. Either way, ignoring the Grimsbanes' eccentricity was an admittedly difficult task. After all, Grimsbane men always wore bike helmets, bulletproof vests, and elbow pads. They constantly looked over their shoulders, jumped at loud noises, and fearfully clutched onto railings, as if afraid the staircase would slip out from under them. The Grimsbane women, in contrast, would sooner start a barroom brawl than hold on to a railing. They wore leather jackets, cussed loudly in public, disappeared for great lengths of time, and often returned to Witchless sporting a myriad of injuries ranging from infected bites to missing limbs.

If Anna ever lost a limb, she'd make her prosthetic red to match her skateboard.

Soon the Grimsbane Family Funeral Home—an imposing, four-story, antebellum-style mansion straight out of an old-timey movie—came into view. Unfortunately, the safety features ruined the image. Forest-green pool noodles encased the ornate wooden railing. Orange cheerleading mats covered the wraparound porch. Soft, overgrown grass brushed Anna's ankles as she skated past the vans and motorcycles that lined the long driveway.

The skateboard slowed. Anna dismounted and picked it up, making her way to the front door. As her hand reached out to open it, a tingle sprang up on the back of her neck—like someone was standing behind her, barely an inch away. Anna spun around, expecting to see an annoying trespasser she'd have to tell off.

But the yard was completely empty, silent aside from the rustling grass, the leaves skittering across the drive, and the faint whispering of the wind.

Anna rubbed the back of her neck. She stared at the deserted space, listening to the strange sounds of autumn.

She could have *sworn* she heard someone breathing.

After a moment, Anna shrugged and opened the door. Maybe she'd imagined it.

The ever-present scent of flowers and formaldehyde hit Anna the second she stepped into the silent foyer. It was always quiet, because everything—the maroon furniture, the coffee-colored carpet, even the slowly revolving ceiling fan—was plush and cushioned, ensuring that if there were ever an accident, something would soften the blow.

If the Grimsbanes knew anything, it was that serious injury was better than death.

Taking her skateboard with her, Anna continued to the door beside the stairs. She briefly glanced at the Grimsbane family crest directly above it: two blood-stained axes forming an X, with the family motto written just beneath in elegant, scrolling script: *Engage. Incapacitate. Kill.*

Anna knocked.

"Coming!" shouted someone, followed by a series of thuds.

The door swung open, revealing Anna's sixteen-year-old sister Madeline, who resembled Wednesday Addams if Wednesday Addams spent a great deal of time throwing knives, lifting weights, and sticking it to the man. Madeline examined Anna as if she were smeared dog poop stuck to the bottom of her combat boots.

Anna stood on her toes, peering over Madeline's shoulder down the only non-plush staircase in the house. Her female relatives' shouts and laughter echoed from the basement, mingling with the familiar scent of lavender and the distinct chorus of the Mamas & the Papas' "California Dreamin.'"

"Coffee?" asked Madeline, holding out a perfectly French-manicured hand.

"Not just yet," Anna said, maneuvering the coffee tote behind her back.

Madeline raised an eyebrow but otherwise didn't say anything.

"I think you, and everyone else"—Anna glanced down the stairs—"might have noticed I've been making the coffee runs in record time for the last few weeks. I've kept everyone's bags stocked, made two new batches of lavender water well in advance of Halloween, and even alphabetized our records. You might say that I'm mature for my age. You might even say that though I'm *physically* twelve, my mind, body, and soul are sixteen. Therefore, I should start hunting ahead of schedule."

"No."

"*Why not?*" Anna complained, falling back to her heels as all thoughts of prepped speeches and rehearsed lines fell tumbling from her brain. "I brought the coffee *so* quickly! I'm fast! Naturally agile! One of the *many* reasons I should be allowed down."

"How many times do we have to tell you you're too young to train?" asked Madeline, snatching the coffee tote from Anna's hands with near-inhuman swiftness.

"I am *not* 'too young'!" Anna shouted, so sick of hearing that stupid phrase.

Madeline sighed. "If you really want to help—"

"No."

"My backpack needs refilling—"

"*No!*"

"Aunt Jane and I are going to Ohio tonight to hunt a witch. We'll need iron bullets, salt bombs—"

"I'm not helping you refill your stupid backpack!" yelled Anna. "I can help with the actual stuff! I want to help break the curse!"

"Backpack refilling is actual stuff that can help break the curse, moron."

Anna crossed her arms, staring into her older sister's dark eyes with the utmost malice. Madeline knew exactly what she was doing—she was torturing Anna by refusing to let her downstairs. And based on the way Madeline was smirking, she thought it was funny, which only made Anna angrier.

Anna darted forward.

Madeline blocked her path easily. She punched Anna in the chest, sending her stumbling backward into the mint-and-tissue table.

"You think you're ready to be a hunter?" asked Madeline, scoffing. "You couldn't kill a Sasquatch."

Before Anna could retort, Madeline slammed the door, leaving Anna cut off from the rest of the family witch hunters. As usual.

Anna thumped the door. "JERK!"

She rubbed her sternum. It hurt a lot more than she'd like to admit.

Another shout of laughter echoed from the basement. Anna's heart clenched in a way that had nothing to do with Madeline's punch.

Would it really have been so bad for the family to let her help?

Anna turned away from the door and started upstairs toward the attic. The bag of scones was somewhat smooshed, but she knew Billy—the only member of the family who never doubted Anna and her abilities—wouldn't mind.

When Anna got to the attic landing, she threw open the door on the right side of the hall, revealing her tiny bedroom. The brick-colored paint and sloped ceiling were barely visible behind posters that featured the stars of *Vampires of West Grove High* and famous American witch hunters. Discarded clothing, pencil drawings of cryptids, and empty Gatorade bottles covered every visible surface. Despite the mess, each cluttered inch of this bedroom was as familiar to Anna as the back of her hand.

Billy sat in a cushy brown armchair beside the circular window overlooking the front lawn, wearing his usual sweater, jeans, and lace-up old-man boots. Like Madeline and Anna, Billy possessed Dad's spindly, spidery appearance, though only he had inherited Mom's freckles and auburn hair, which almost seemed to glow in the soft, yellow light of the reading lamp. He was reading a worn-out paperback copy of *The King of the Jewels* that was studded with colorful sticky notes.

"It didn't work!" shouted Anna, setting down her skateboard and slumping onto her twin bed. She shrugged off her leather jacket and threw it on the floor. "They *still* won't let me downstairs."

"Really?" asked Billy, placing a bookmark to save his page. "You said what I told you to say, right? All about your mind, body, and soul being more mature than your actual numerical age?"

"I tried to." Anna fished through the bag for a pumpkin scone and tossed it to Billy.

The scone bounced off Billy's finger and nearly fell on the floor. He barely caught it with his other hand. "So what happened?"

"Madeline."

Billy huffed. "Of course."

"I *twied* to get *pathst* her," Anna explained through a mouthful of cinnamon scone, "but she blocked me. She wouldn't listen to a *word* I had to say."

"They never do," said Billy, taking a bite out of his scone.

"So, I'm guessing things didn't go well with Mom and Dad?"

Billy had been trying to convince Mom and Dad to let him stay in school for weeks, to no avail. Like all the other Grimsbane men, Billy was going to be pulled out of school when he turned thirteen. Between bullies and gym class and all the other dangers that came with middle school, it was just too unsafe to educate the Grimsbane boys in a traditional manner once the curse set in. Though Anna recognized that Billy would be endangered if he kept going to school with her, she hated the idea of leaving him behind.

"Same old, same old," said Billy. "It's all 'too dangerous' and 'going to kill me even if I'm careful.'" Billy made mocking air quotes with his fingers, rolling his eyes. "They're determined to homeschool me. They want me to start working in the funeral home as soon as possible. You think Dad would understand, seeing as he got cursed when he turned thirteen too, but no! He's just as bad as everyone else. Based on the current, deplorable state of our communications, it looks like I'm going to end up handing out tissues and recommending headstone designs forever."

"Don't say that. There's still plenty of time until . . ." Anna sat up, struggling to find the right words, not wanting to come out and say it. *"You know."*

"I get cursed to die a horrible, miserable death?"

Anna sighed. He'd said it. "You don't need to be so casual about it."

"Well, there's no point in teetering around the issue. I'm well aware of my impending doom." Billy stood up and sat down beside Anna, taking the scone bag from her hands. "It's just"—he sighed—"I was kind of expecting the curse to be broken by now."

"It still might get broken before our birthday," Anna assured him, "especially if I can convince the family to let me help out." Though the Watcher—the witch who had cursed their family—was the most dangerous witch in history, Anna was certain that, given the chance, she could take the Watcher down quickly and easily, largely due to the excessive amount of time she'd spent studying witches and using practice weapons in her bedroom—eager to try out the real-deal stuff when she was older.

"You *really* think you'd be able to hunt the Watcher in seven days?" asked Billy.

"For sure," answered Anna confidently. "I know everything there is to know about hunting."

"I wouldn't say you know *everything*."

"Please," said Anna, holding up a hand. "Gimme a few questions."

Billy sighed but played along. "Where was the Mothman first spotted?"

"Point Pleasant, West Virginia, in 1966," Anna recited from memory, a perfect image of the flash card she'd made clear in her mind. She turned back to Billy. "But that's an easy one."

"Which weapons can kill witches?"

"Again, easy, and also a trick question. You need salt, kindling, and a lighter. Only fire can kill witches."

"And what are three alternative names for Ozark Howlers?"

"Devil Cat, Black Howler, and . . ." Anna furrowed her brow. She could picture the flash card in her mind—light purple, with Mom's scrawled handwriting written across it. Why couldn't she picture the last name for an Ozark Howler?

"Nightshade Bear?" finished Billy.

"Yeah, a Nightshade Bear!" Anna smiled. "I totally knew that."

"Sure you did."

Anna shoved him with her shoulder so hard, he nearly fell off the bed, but nonetheless laughed. "Even with my lack of your *school brains*, I *do* know everything about the Watcher. That's why I'll be the greatest hunter of all time, as soon as the family lets me downstairs."

Before Billy could respond, Dad shouted the two most dreaded words in the world up the staircase.

"FAMILY MEETING!"

The words hung in the air as if made of fog. Anna's mind began to spiral—memories of every bad thing she'd done in the last few months rising to the top of her consciousness. She and Billy didn't exactly have the best conduct record. If Principal Myers had sent a note home about the water fountain incident (they'd meant for the water to shoot their friend's bully in the face, *not* an elderly teacher just months away from retirement), or had somehow discovered that the twins were the ones who had set off the stink bombs before the football rally, or even had found out about Operation Bullfrog Breakout (carried out seamlessly just before dissection day), the twins were going to be in *serious* trouble.

Oh God. Mom and Dad were going to kill her.

Billy was growing paler by the second. "We better get downstairs," he said quickly, standing up. "We'll be in even more trouble if we're late."

2

The Morbid Meeting

Grimsbane family meetings tended to be peculiar affairs, as they were usually held in front of a casket.

This particular meeting was no different. The Grand Viewing Room, the biggest room in the house, was the easiest place for all the Grimsbanes to gather at once. The chairs were already neatly arranged, so Mom, Dad, Grandma, or any other angry adult could stand at the front of the room and berate the offending family member until they felt proper shame for their actions. With Mr. Carmichael's funeral in just two hours, the Grimsbanes had to have the meeting with his corpse laid out neatly in the velvet-lined coffin before them.

There were about eighty wooden folding chairs covered in plush, tartan fabric on either side of the room. The Grimsbanes occupied over half of them. A trio of burly aunts sat in the front row, whispering in hushed tones. Beside them, an uncle leaned against a window, reading a Stephen King novel. Madeline sat on the left side of the aisle, complaining about something to a few of the older cousins, who were clearly trying their best to resist shoving Madeline's eyeliner up her perfectly contoured nose.

Anna grabbed Billy's arm and pulled him firmly to the right side of the room, where they took their seats.

"Anna!" someone shouted. "Billy!"

The twins turned. Two shivering, ectoplasm-covered cousins, clearly just back from a ghost hunt, sat on the other side of the aisle. They were wrapped in several layers of flannel blankets—trying to stave off the freezing chill of Ghost Lurgy (symptoms including, but not limited to, emotional distress, dulled senses, intrusive thoughts, low body temperature, and indigestion).

"What?" asked Anna, leaning over Billy's chair to talk.

One cousin said something, but Anna didn't catch it over the Grimsbanes' chatter.

"What?" Billy repeated, pointing to his ear.

The other cupped her hands around her mouth and yelled, but Anna still couldn't hear what she was saying.

"WHAT?" Anna asked.

"WAS IT YOU?" the cousins shouted in unison.

The back door of the parlor slammed open, as if kicked by a cowboy.

Anna turned and saw Mom and Dad enter, bringing with them a cold wind that swept the energy from the room. Though they were normally affectionate, Mom and Dad could be intimidating when they wanted to be, especially when wearing their black funeral suits. Even with the oddness of Dad's helmet and bulletproof vest, they seemed like harbingers of death.

Anna *really* hoped she and Billy weren't the ones in trouble, but based on the cousins' question, it was more than likely that this meeting was about something the twins had done. Anna gulped as Mom and Dad took their places at the front of the crowd.

"Thank you all for gathering on such short notice," said Dad, straightening his suit jacket as he turned to Mom. "Shall we get the standard business out of the way?"

"Exactly what I was thinking," said Mom, turning to the folder in her hand. "First things first: Halloween preparations."

The women in the room sat up straighter. Anna felt her stomach twist. Great. She was going to have to wait to find out if she was in trouble. "Standard business" could take ages if there was a disagreement.

"It goes without saying that Halloween is the most dangerous night of the year for any hunting family," said Mom. "Witches get more powerful on Halloween, drawing cryptids and ghosts from whatever region they're in closer to them. This is especially true of the Watcher. If you see anyone enter the Not-So-Witchless Woods after dark, be sure to let the family know so the hunters can collect them before they get mauled by the Nain Rouge, the Dover Demon, a grassman, or—well, you get the idea."

Anna couldn't help the shiver that rolled through her at the mention of the terrifying creatures that traveled to the Not-So-Witchless Woods every Halloween—demonic imps, ravenous hellhounds, cannibalistic monsters with an insatiable desire for human flesh. Some cryptids were deadlier than others. Only the most experienced hunters could go after them, and oftentimes, even those hunters didn't return home.

"We're going to double the patrols we had going last year," Mom continued, "which will require double the weapons: iron bullets, salt bombs—all of it. We need everything in tip-top shape by the end of the week."

"Fellas, you know the drill for Halloween," said Dad.

"Stay safe. Stay inside," the men in the room all echoed.

Anna noticed Billy tense at the familiar phrase. His knee bounced up and down like he was trying to stomp a hole through the carpet.

"Next order of business," continued Dad, "the tourists."

A great, mumbling complaint arose from the room. Tourists had a tendency to crowd around the Grimsbane Family Funeral Home to take pictures and stop Grimsbanes to ask if the curse was, "just like the one in the movie *The Watcher in the Woods.*" Anna was more than willing to give them an answer for the right price, usually around twenty bucks.

"I know they can be annoying," said Dad, "but remember the business they bring is good for Witchless. That being said, try to avoid interacting with the tourists—especially anyone involved with the Spook

Caboose, Late-Night Murder Tours, or the Grim Tales of the Grimsbanes. Don't give interviews to the press. Don't offer tours of the funeral home. I am speaking directly to you, Jasper."

Dad's troublemaker brother-in-law, Anna's uncle Jasper, held up a hand. "Guilty as charged!" He guffawed at his own joke, slapping one of his knee pads.

"And on to our final bit of business," said Mom in her disappointed voice. "We've called this meeting under less than pleasant circumstances."

Anna braced herself. This was it. She and Billy were totally done for!

Mom sighed heavily and placed her hands on her hips. "As everyone is well aware, things have a tendency to go missing from our storerooms—bottles of lavender water, salt bombs, the occasional practice weapon. This we can chalk up to disorganization—something we all need to work on."

Anna let out a sigh of relief. The meeting wasn't about anything she and Billy had done at school. She smiled slightly, holding out a hand for Billy to low-five. He did so. They leaned back and crossed their arms, ready to ride out the rest of the meeting in peace.

"Unfortunately," continued Mom, "this disorganization has taken a dire turn. Diligence's diary is missing."

All sense of peace vanished with a poof. The family broke into scandalized chatter. Grandma clutched her chest like she was going to have a heart attack. An uncle nearly collapsed from the shock. An aunt was barely able to catch him, guiding him to a chair while a cousin fanned him with a funeral pamphlet.

Anna herself couldn't believe what she was hearing. Diligence's diary was the most important book in their family library. It was the record of all the witches, ghosts, and cryptids the family had encountered since they started hunting, originally created by the first hunter in their family—Diligence Grimsbane. Every girl in the family—well, every girl besides Anna—had to read it cover to cover when they started training. No one was allowed to take it out of the storage room— not even Grandma! How could it have gone missing?

Dad held up a hand, and the chatter ceased. "Now, we're not blaming anyone for this. Surely, someone took the diary from the library and forgot to put it back. If anyone forgot to return it, I recommend they let us know now so we can put this unfortunate business behind us."

Anna looked around at her relatives, meeting several furtive eyes, waiting to see if anyone fessed up.

Mom put her hands on her hips. "In that case,

everyone please keep a sharp eye out for the diary. Losing it means losing the bulk of our family's recorded knowledge, which would be nearly impossible to get back."

The crowd remained silent.

"Well," said Dad, clasping his hands together, "if no one has any questions, we can all go about our—"

"I have a question!" blurted Billy, raising his hand.

In one swift motion, every head in the room swiveled to face him.

Anna turned to her brother, open-mouthed and wide-eyed as a fish. Billy—smart and extroverted as he was—*never* talked during family meetings. There was an unspoken rule that *neither* of them talked to avoid drawing attention to any misdeeds or mishaps they might have caused. Why was he breaking this rule now?

Billy cleared his throat before he stood up. "Uh, since everyone's here, I thought we could put the issue of me staying in school up to a vote."

Somehow Anna's jaw managed to drop even farther. What was Billy thinking? He knew how dangerous school would become once the curse set in. Plus, the idea of putting the matter up to a vote was laughable. No one would ever vote in *favor* of Billy risking death.

The other Grimsbanes, it seemed, felt the same way.

"SHAME ON YOU, WILLIAM!" shouted an uncle.

"DON'T YOU VALUE YOUR OWN LIFE?" screamed a cousin.

Billy struggled to talk over the shouting crowd. "Look! Look! I know it's an unpopular idea, but why can't I keep going to school if I take precautions?"

"Billy," said Anna, tugging on his shirt to pull him down. "This is a bad idea."

Billy shrugged her off. Anna's brow furrowed. Billy had never ignored her like that before. What was going on with him?

"Precautions?" Dad asked. The crowd started to quiet down. "What exactly do you mean by that, son?"

Billy shrugged. "I don't know." His voice cracked, and he coughed. "I mean, I'd wear a helmet and knee pads—"

The Grimsbanes exploded into protests.

"Think about it!" Billy shouted. "I mean *really* think about it! We should at least *try* sending me to school as a trial run! I promise I'll be careful!"

"Jonathan Grimsbane said the same thing when he joined the Revolutionary War!" said Dad. "And where did he end up?"

"Stabbed in the buttocks with a bayonet, got an infection, and died!" shouted a Grimsbane in the crowd.

"And what about George Grimsbane, who decided to go dancing during the Roaring Twenties?"

"Sprained his ankle while dancing the Charleston, fell off the stage, and died!"

"And who could forget Bobby Grimsbane, who wanted to try all the trends of the nineties? Anyone remember what happened to him?"

"Tripped on a Skip-It, hit his head on the pavement, and died!"

"Okay, okay," said Billy, cutting off Dad before he could continue. "I know how the curse works. The Watcher told Reverend Perseverance Grimsbane that any men connected to his bloodline would die sudden and unusual deaths, and for the last three hundred forty years, we've all died sudden and unusual deaths. Here's the thing, though." Billy paused like a crazed scientist about to explain a wild theory. "I'm going to die a sudden and unusual death no matter what I do!"

Anna winced. She didn't even want to think about that.

"I'm going to choke on a pen cap or slip on a banana peel and crack my head open or something weird like that!" Billy continued. "So why shouldn't I keep going to school?"

"Because it's an unnecessary risk that will shorten your life," said Mom plainly, her stoic demeanor unshaken.

"But Anna gets to go!" protested Billy, gesturing to her.

Anna recoiled as several eyes snapped to her. Now he was dragging her into this?

"In case you've forgotten," interjected Madeline, "Anna's not cursed." She leaned back, crossing her muscular arms. "It's pretty simple, my dude. If you go to school after your birthday, you'll die."

For once, Anna had to agree with her sister.

"Anna?" asked Billy, turning to Anna and giving her a look that said, *Back me up, here!*

Anna's breath hitched. Every instinct she had told her to support Billy. However, there was *no way* Billy could keep going to school once he got cursed. It would be too dangerous. Besides, he could still go to school online. Sure, working in the funeral home wasn't exactly an adventurous life, but it was a safe one, and Anna wanted to keep Billy safe.

"I mean . . ." Anna rubbed the back of her neck. She trailed off awkwardly. There wasn't a good answer.

Every single one would upset Billy. "I don't know, man."

Billy took a slight step back, confusion crossing his face for a second before he turned violently back to Mom and Dad. "You can't stop me from going to school! I'm only in seventh grade! My life just . . ." Billy ran his hand through his hair, a pained expression on his face. "It can't be over yet! This isn't fair!"

The Grimsbanes were silent. Anna's heart twisted itself into knots, whirling and writhing in her chest. She hated seeing Billy upset. Anna desperately wanted to help him. Unfortunately, Anna wasn't *allowed* to help because of the family rule that prevented girls from hunting until their sixteenth birthday. Anna and Billy agreed on one thing at least: everything about this was unfair.

"No one said it was fair," said Dad, his voice suddenly softer. "Believe me, I know how you feel. I wanted to keep going to school when I was your age, but that wasn't in the cards for me. It wasn't in the cards for any of us." Dad gestured to the other men in the room. "Regardless of the fairness of the situation, you can't go to school once the curse sets in."

Billy glared malevolently at Mom and Dad, as if attempting to melt them through sheer force of will.

He clenched his fists so tightly, his hands were turning white.

It was then that Great-Grandma Lenore stood up.

Despite being a heavily scarred, heavily wrinkled eighty-nine-year-old, Great-Grandma Lenore was easily the most intimidating person Anna had ever met. She handed the hot pink tomahawk sheath she was knitting to Grandma, drew herself up to her full height, and turned to face Billy.

With a shaking hand, she reached forward and pointed to him.

"If you—" she said in a croaking voice. "If you take *any* risks after you turn thirteen, you will die."

"But—"

A quick glare from Dad snapped Billy's mouth shut.

Great-Grandma Lenore clutched Grandma's arm for support. "Horrible, horrible things happen to Grimsbane men who don't take the curse seriously!" She swallowed, then stated in a voice barely above a whisper, "Therefore, you must leave the curse breaking to the women. Hope we find the Watcher. Hope we fulfill the goal set by our founding matriarch Diligence Grimsbane. Hope we succeed in our mission of killing the witch and ending the curse, and killing every other witch, ghost, and cryptid who threatens the safety of humans. Until the women break the Watcher's curse, you must not take any risks."

Billy's face fell as quickly as a light bulb blowing. He turned violently back to Mom and Dad. "I'm going to stay in school, and there is nothing anyone can do to stop me."

With that, Billy stormed out of the room, leaving a sea of groaning Grimsbanes behind him. Anna stood and followed. She knew Billy better than anyone, and if he was upset, she was determined to make him feel better.

"Chestnut wood for his coffin, I think," muttered an uncle. "It would suit Billy's complexion quite nicely."

3

Awful Accusations

Anna thudded up the stairs to the attic, determined to reach Billy's bedroom before anyone else. She turned to the bedroom door directly across from hers—adorned in posters from *The King of the Jewels*, Monsters and Mayhem, *Is That a Faun in My Wardrobe?*, and other nerdy stuff that Anna had no interest in—and rapped on it as hard as she could.

"Go away, Anna," Billy said. His voice sounded heavier than usual.

Anna ignored him, continuing to knock on the door.

"GO—AWAY!" Billy shouted.

Anna rolled her eyes. She stopped knocking,

29

reached into her back pocket, and pulled out a bobby pin—an essential tool she always kept on her person. Anna stuck the bobby pin into the lock on his door and began fiddling with it.

"Anna, don't!" Billy yelled. She heard him stumble as he got up then heard the scrape of furniture against the floor.

The lock clicked open. Anna leapt up and attempted to throw the door ajar, but it was quickly intercepted by Billy, who attempted to shove it closed.

"Let—me—in!" Anna said, shoving harder on the door.

"I don't want to talk!" yelled Billy.

"Oh, so *now* you don't want to talk?"

"What's that supposed to mean?"

"That you did a ton of talking during the family meeting!" Anna struggled to push the door open. Why was this so difficult? Anna was the more athletic of the twins. Why was Billy suddenly just as strong as she was?

"I don't want to talk about the meeting!" Billy said. "Just leave me alone!"

Anna took a deep breath. Desperate times called for desperate measures. She threw her left foot between the door and the door frame and let go. With all the force on her side suddenly gone, the door went swinging against her foot with a thick THUMP. Anna felt pain jolt through the arch.

"Oh my God, are you okay?" asked Billy, throwing open the door. "I didn't mean to do that! I just—" He looked up and saw Anna's smiling face. He glowered at her, and Anna noticed his eyes were red-rimmed. He'd clearly been crying, but Anna wasn't going to mention it. "Oh, you—"

"Gotcha," said Anna, raising her eyebrows twice. She hobbled past him. Billy's room looked almost exactly like Anna's, just far more orderly, and facing the forest rather than the front yard. It also featured a rather heavy wooden bookshelf that housed an army of well-worn paperbacks. Anna felt a pang of sadness as she realized this bookshelf would likely be too unsafe to keep in here once Billy turned thirteen. There was a chance it could fall over and crush him. He'd have to find another place to store his books.

"That was a cheap trick," said Billy, crossing his arms and leaning against the door frame.

Anna threw herself back onto Billy's bed. "You should've seen it coming."

He sighed. "So what do you want?"

"Take a wild guess," said Anna. "You ran up here

all upset after causing a huge scene at the meeting. Diligence's diary is missing, so Halloween just got, like, ten times more dangerous for the family, but you, for some reason, decided to pitch the idea of you staying in school while everyone was still losing it about the diary."

"I had to!" Billy chimed. "I mean, don't you think I should go to school?"

Anna paused. There was a time she genuinely thought she and Billy would never have to deal with this—that the curse would be broken before their birthday—that things could go on as normal, but that wasn't how their lives were turning out. "We're going to be thirteen, Billy. There's nothing we can do about it."

"I know that," said Billy, throwing his hands up. "Believe me, I know that! It's all I've been able to think about!"

"I get it—"

"No you don't!" shouted Billy. "It's different for you! When you grow up, you get to become a witch hunter and go on amazing quests and build a whole legacy that's going to last generations! Me? What do I get to do besides 'stay inside' and 'stay safe'?" His voice grew hoarse at the last word, and he swallowed. "I'm not ready to give up my life. You don't understand how I feel."

Anna sat in the silence for a moment. She hadn't really thought about it like that. She was so excited to grow up and become a witch hunter. How would she have felt if she were the cursed one? If she had to give up school and skateboarding and all the stuff that she liked doing?

Anna crossed her legs. "It's just like everyone else said, Billy. This isn't fair. I don't want to go to school without you. I don't want us to be separated. I want to go on adventures *with you*, but we can't—not until someone breaks the curse." *And that won't happen until the family lets me hunt.*

Billy sighed deeply, dropped his head, and slid down the door frame until he was sitting on the floor. He put his head between his knees. "This sucks."

Anna nodded. That was a pretty good summary of the situation.

Anna got up from the bed and sat beside Billy. She put her hand on his shoulder. They sat there like that for a moment. Anna couldn't help but feel the anxiety and fear creeping over her. Billy was clumsy now, but it would get a million times worse once he turned thirteen. He could die at any second. She couldn't think of anything more terrifying than that.

"I wish I could do something to help," Anna said.

Billy opened his mouth to speak, then closed it again, before taking a deep breath. "I wish you could too."

An idea popped into Anna's head. "You know what might *really* help the situation?"

Billy raised his eyebrows expectantly.

"Pancakes," said Anna.

Billy blinked. He looked Anna up and down, a curious expression on his face, almost like he was seeing her for the first time. "Pancakes? After all that, you're suggesting *pancakes*? That's your big solution to this problem?"

Anna shrugged. "I like pancakes."

Specifically, she liked the Blue Moon Diner—an all-day-breakfast restaurant located just across the street from the funeral home. It was run by their friend Rosario's family. The Blue Moon was home to the best pancakes in Witchless, and was the best place to get cheered up on a bad day.

Anna sighed. "I *guess* we can sit here and wait till Mom and Dad decide how they're going to approach the family meeting incident. I'm sure they'll have a lot to say about—"

"I'll get my coat," Billy said quickly.

* * *

A few moments later, Anna and Billy were coated up and ready to walk across the street. Passing through the foyer, Anna noticed Madeline and her older cousin Camille crowded around the window beside the front door, whispering in hushed tones and pointing at something outside.

Anna was set on ignoring them until Madeline giggled in a very un-Madeline-like fashion.

Anna and Billy exchanged a surprised look, spun on their heels, and approached the window. Anna stood on a step so she could see around her taller relatives. "What's going on?"

"Oh, nothing," said Camille, flipping her blond braids over her shoulder.

Anna huffed and followed her older cousin's gaze, landing upon a muscular teenager with a chiseled jawline, dark brown skin, and close-cropped black hair—Rosario's oldest brother, Salvador. He was shirtless and playing basketball in his front yard with some of his equally shirtless friends, all of whom were seniors at Madeline's high school.

Anna turned from Madeline to Salvador, then back to Madeline.

"You have a crush on *Salvador*?" asked Anna.

Madeline rolled her eyes. "I'd mind my business, if

I were you. Wouldn't want me to tell Mom about you stealing the diary."

Anna furrowed her brow. "Huh?"

"Oh, don't pretend you didn't do it," snarled Camille. "Diligence's diary somehow just happens to go missing right before Halloween?"

Madeline smirked. "A stupid mistake that could only be made by the world's biggest moron—a wannabe witch hunter with access to the storeroom library." Madeline narrowed her gaze viciously at Anna. "You wouldn't happen to know any wannabee hunters with access to the storeroom library, would you?"

Anna wasn't entirely sure what Madeline was asking, until she realized that Madeline was accusing *her* of stealing Diligence's diary from the family library.

"Anna didn't steal the diary!" protested Billy, immediately coming to Anna's defense. Despite Anna's anger and confusion about the situation, she couldn't help but feel a bit guilty. She'd failed to defend Billy at the family meeting, but that didn't stop him from helping her out now.

"She definitely took it," Camille growled. "If not her, who else?"

Anna sputtered in anger. "I'd never—I want to be a hunter, but I'd never steal something important!"

Madeline sighed, turning to face the window. "Why don't you stop seeking attention, put the diary back where it belongs, and leave us alone?"

Anna crossed her arms and glared at her older sister. She couldn't believe Madeline's nerve. Anna might have been a wannabe witch hunter, but she'd never steal Diligence's diary, and she certainly wasn't an attention-seeker. She hated Madeline from the top of her perfectly straight hair to the tips of her perfectly painted toes.

In a moment of pure animal instinct, Anna lost all thought, drew her hand back, and walloped Madeline in the back of the head.

"RUN FOR IT!" Anna screamed.

Without registering the string of swear words exploding from Madeline's mouth, Anna took off running to the front door with Billy close behind her, hoping with all her might that Madeline would have enough sense not to beat Anna up in front of her crush.

4

Perils and Pancakes

Anna made her way down the driveway, trying to catch her breath as Billy trailed behind her. Anna looked over her shoulder. Madeline and Camille were glaring at her from the window. Madeline drew a finger over her throat, and Anna turned immediately back to Billy as he caught up to her. "You know I didn't steal Diligence's diary, right?"

"Of course," said Billy. "I mean, you could just read the diary if you wanted to, right? So what's the point in stealing it?"

"Well, no. I'm actually not allowed to read it," said Anna, shoving her hands in her pockets. "I mean, I *could*, but I'm not supposed to." She took a few more steps. "Okay, so I snuck a peek here and there, and maybe I spent a few hours reading it this summer when everyone was out on a big hunt, but it's an *awesome* book! There's so much information in there about all kinds of stuff—literally every cool hunt our family's been on for over three hundred years, but I'd never *actually* steal it. It's too important."

"I know," Billy said. "You don't have to convince me."

"Who do you think stole it, then?" Anna asked. She ran over her relatives in her mind. The men never went into the storeroom (salt bombs and death curses didn't mix well). The women valued the diary too much to lose track of it.

"I don't think anyone stole it," said Billy. "It was probably an accident. Someone must have slipped it into their bag while their mind was on other things. When they discover their mistake, they'll return it."

"You *really* think that could've happened?" asked Anna. Everyone was always *so* cautious around the diary.

Billy nodded. "It's way more likely that the diary was misplaced than stolen."

"Stolen?" called a tourist taking a selfie by the funeral home sign. "What was stolen?"

"Mind your business!" called Anna and Billy in unison as they crossed the street.

The Ortiz-Riveras lived in an unkempt, medium-sized Victorian house just across the street from the funeral home. Rosario's moms held a liberal point of view when it came to plants and nature, so they let the wildflowers, weeds, and grass in the yard grow as tall as they pleased. Ms. Ortiz and Ms. Rivera also had eight adopted children. As a result, tasks like fixing the shingles and putting another layer of mulberry paint on the house to cover up where it was peeling fell quite low on their to-do list. Christmas lights hung on the wraparound porch, and were turned on from January until December. Just above the porch, there was a neon sign featuring a blue moon sitting upon a stack of pancakes above the glowing, yellow words THE BLUE MOON DINER. Beneath that was a far less enchanting poster board with the message *Daily yoga class @ 6 p.m. Inquire inside!* written across it in bleeding black Sharpie.

"Hey, guys!" called Salvador as Anna and Billy passed. "How's it goin'?"

Anna and Billy made a big show of waving at him, knowing it would drive Madeline nuts.

"See?" Anna asked Billy as they approached. "Aren't you already feeling better?"

"Not really," he grumbled.

"Already feeling better!" shouted Anna as she walked in the front door, pulling Billy in behind her as the door chimed to signal someone's entrance.

The inside of Rosario's house was nearly as strange as the Grimsbanes'. Plants of all varieties wove their way across the ceiling and walls. Ornately designed vintage rugs covered every inch of the floor, layered upon one another haphazardly like papers scattered upon a desk. Tapestries featuring diagrams of hands and celestial bodies dotted the walls. Several people sat at booths, tables, and high-tops littered about the foyer, each accompanied by a colorful tablecloth. To the right, there was a swinging set of double doors leading to the kitchen. To the left, there was a door covered in flowing veils, leading to the yoga studio.

Even from the entrance, Anna could hear her and Billy's two best friends bickering from their usual booth in the corner. Suvi Kumar and Rosario Ortiz-Rivera were among the only middle schoolers in Witchless who still wholeheartedly believed the stories about witches, cryptids, and curses that the Grimsbanes knew to be true. Naturally, Suvi and Rosario fell into the same "misfit" category that Anna and Billy did. This, coupled with the fact that Suvi, Rosario, and the Grimsbane twins had all lived on the same street since they were in preschool, made them incredibly close friends.

Anna walked to Suvi and Rosario's booth, pulling Billy behind her.

"It's really not a big deal," Suvi, a copper-skinned girl with thick, shoulder-length hair and a mouth full of braces, was saying to Rosario.

"You need to explain your point of view and tell him he's hurting your feelings," said Rosario, a soft-spoken girl with olive skin, a sturdy, athletic build, and a voluminous cascade of dark curls. "That'll solve it."

"What's going on?" asked Anna, sliding into the booth beside Suvi.

Rosario sighed deeply. "It appears that Wharton has struck again."

"Neil Wharton?" Billy asked, sitting next to Rosario.

Suvi's quick glance downward was enough of an answer.

Ever since Suvi's dad died last spring, Suvi had doubled down on discussing the latest theories surrounding the supernatural on her YouTube channel, *Ghouligans*. Unfortunately, the only thing she'd gained from the extra effort was an impressive following of trolls, both online and in real life. This included Neil Wharton—the biggest, meanest kid in Witchless, who attended the fancy private school that Mrs. Kumar insisted Suvi attend, despite all of Suvi's neighborhood friends attending public school.

Rosario tossed Anna a book—Suvi's most recent read. It was covered in scribbles and was browning and curling up at the edges like a dead cockroach.

Billy took it from Anna's hands, his face screwed up in disgust. "What kind of monster would do this to a book?"

"What happened?" asked Anna.

"Water damage," explained Rosario.

"Dude," said Anna seriously to Suvi, "you've got to start sticking up for yourself!"

Suvi shook her head. "I don't want to cause any trouble."

"You aren't causing any trouble," Billy assured her, gesturing to the book. "This is all Wharton's fault. He's ruining your stuff."

Anna nodded heartily in agreement. "One swift punch to the nose, problem solved! That stupid jerk won't know what hit him!"

Rosario held up a finger. "I hate to interject, but shouldn't fighting be the last resort? I mean, how would you feel if someone ran up to you and punched you in the nose for something you didn't even realize you were doing?"

"You don't think Wharton realizes he's been scribbling all over Suvi's stuff?" asked Billy.

"Maybe not. That's why Suvi should talk to him first. It might be a big misunderstanding."

"Time for talking's over," said Anna. "It's time to fight."

"Anna, be honest. Do I look like the fighting type?" Suvi gestured to her scrawny form, holding out her hands expectantly.

Suvi didn't, but Anna wasn't going to let her gain any ground. "Fine, I'll do it. I can sneak out of my school, break into your school—"

"I appreciate the offer, but the real way to show them I'm not weird is to prove that ghosts exist—"

"—you call me on the walkie-talkies, tell me where the bullies are, and I'll handle everything! You don't even need to be there!"

Rosario shook her head disapprovingly. "Suvi, you and Wharton need to sit down and talk it out. He'll stop if you calmly explain to him that he's making you sad. No one wants to make anyone else feel sad. I can mediate the conversation if you want me to. I'm *really* good at mediation."

Anna nearly screamed in frustration. The older Grimsbane boys—and soon Billy—were natural targets for bullying. As a result, Anna was an expert at handling mean kids. Admittedly, Anna's method of handling bullies involved throwing their insults right back at them, along with a few well-placed punches. That usually shut them up, even if it did land her in detention.

"Just . . ." Anna grasped desperately for the right thing to say. "Just don't take any of Wharton's garbage, okay?"

Suvi took a deep breath. "I'll think about it."

"So, where have you two been?" Rosario asked the twins, clearly all too eager to change the topic from anything contentious.

"Just counting down the days to my impending demise," said Billy, crossing his arms and leaning back.

Before anyone could respond, a familiar figure came sliding into view.

"Greetings and salutations, fellow travelers," called Rosario's fifteen-year-old brother Xander as he strode up to their table, tucking a wavy strand of blue hair behind his ear. As usual, he was wearing a grunge outfit straight out of the nineties. He began reading directly off a notepad, as he was required to do when addressing any table, though Xander had made a few modifications to the waitstaff's usual greeting. "My name is Xander, and I'll be your waiter this afternoon. Because this is a pancake restaurant, I recommend the pancakes. Prayer cards do not count as tips. We take both cash and credit. If you try to pay with a check, I'll drown myself in your orange juice. Please don't ask stupid questions. I genuinely hate working here. What can I get you to drink?" Xander looked up from the notepad and grinned. "*Hifen os hilsen*, my dude." He punched Billy in the shoulder.

"*Hifen os hilsen*," Billy responded, making a hand gesture that Anna immediately recognized as the two-fingered elf salute from *The King of the Jewels*.

"You still up for Monsters and Mayhem next week?" Xander asked.

"Next we—" Billy's voice cracked, and he cleared his throat before lowering it considerably below its usual pitch. "I—um—I don't know if next week will work, seeing as I'm getting cursed this week."

"You can't drop out of the campaign!" Suvi shouted suddenly, causing Anna to jump in her seat. "We're just one day of travel away from the sorcerer king's lair! We can't defeat him without you! You're the only healer!"

Billy grimaced. "I mean, your character technically *could* heal if you changed your spells up a little bit."

Rosario and Anna exchanged a pained look as Billy, Suvi, and Xander began to squabble. As much as they loved Billy and Suvi, Anna and Rosario just couldn't wrap their minds around Monsters and Mayhem. It made no sense that anyone would consider a math-based board game fun, especially when everything was made up. Anna preferred the idea of slaying monsters in real life.

"We're having a movie night while they play, right?" Rosario asked.

"Definitely," said Anna. "We'll go over to my place. We can watch *Vampires of West Grove High Two.*"

"And *Vampires of West Grove High One, Extended Edition*?"

Anna nodded enthusiastically. Rosario was the only one of her friends who understood what a masterpiece *Vampires of West Grove High* was. Rosario liked the magic elements. Anna liked the action sequences. Both of them *loved* lead actor Kurt Mackenzie. He played Edmund, a vampire who roamed the halls of

West Grove High School, desperate to find love.

Secretly, Anna was disappointed that vampires were one of the few monsters that *weren't* real.

"Sleepover?" asked Anna.

"Sleepover," Rosario agreed.

Xander slid in next to Billy. "You think I'm letting some stupid curse get in the way of *my* campaign? No way! I've got a fix that's gonna blow your mind." He grabbed both sides of Billy's head and shook it. "Consider, a virtual tabletop." He slung one arm around Billy's shoulders and gestured with the other as if to some impressive landscape. "The whole thing's online, so you don't have to leave your bedroom and, like, risk dying or whatever."

"Oh, I, uh—thanks," Billy stammered, turning about as red as Anna's skateboard. "How's that going to work, though, if I can't, uh, see you?"

"Don't worry, man," Xander assured him. "I've got you covered."

Billy smiled in a rather goofy way. "Right—uh—um—right. Yeah. Definitely."

"In the meantime," said Suvi, turning to the rest of the group. "I've been thinking of ideas for our Halloween costumes."

Anna's eyes widened. With all the stress surrounding Billy's impending curse, she hadn't even considered trick-or-treating. She usually got super excited about it, but now trick-or-treating seemed . . . silly. How could she go door-to-door in a costume begging for candy when so much was going on, especially now that the diary was missing?

Xander scoffed. "You guys are going trick-or-treating? Aren't you a little old for that?"

Anna scowled. Were they too old for trick-or-treating? They were in seventh grade—just two years away from high school. Maybe that's why it seemed silly. Now that she thought about it, she didn't know how she'd feel if any of her classmates saw her running around with a bunch of kindergartners. Even so, trick-or-treating was really fun. She liked free candy and costumes, and she wasn't sure if she wanted to give it up just yet.

"We're not *too old*," Suvi laughed, waving Xander off. "We always go trick-or-treating."

"But we wouldn't be opposed to other Halloween options!" called Billy. "What're—" He attempted to rest his head on his hand, but his elbow missed the table. He righted himself, somehow managing to blush an even deeper shade of red. "Uh, what're *you* doing for Halloween, Xander?"

"We're *definitely* going trick-or-treating," Anna said with an air of finality. "All of us." She glared at Billy.

"We're doing matching costumes as well," said Rosario, nodding firmly at Anna in agreement. "Suvi's a great costume designer. She comes up with the best ideas every year."

"So what are we being this year?" Anna asked Suvi.

"I was thinking maybe fairies."

Anna almost threw up in her mouth.

"Well, that certainly is unique," said Rosario, giving Suvi a forced smile. "We can add that to the drawing board and come up with some alternative options. We have plenty of time!"

Xander rolled his eyes. "Well, if you all decide you want to do something a bit more 'grown-up' this Halloween, seeing as it's Billy's last night of freedom and all, some of the kids in my AV club are having a party. It's at a rich kid's house, too, so you know there's gonna be *choice* snacks."

Anna's mind rushed with excitement. Xander had invited them to a high school party, just like in the movies! But—Anna winced internally—she *really* wanted to go trick-or-treating. She really wanted to do both.

Xander stood up and pointed a pencil at Billy. "Pumpkin waffles." He turned to the others. "Apple cinnamon pancakes for the rest of the group." He smiled, scribbled something on a piece of his notepad paper, ripped it out, and handed it to Billy. "The address. Hope I see you there."

5

All Hallows' Argument

Halloween arrived in a rush of dampness and fog that settled upon Witchless like a wet blanket. Tomorrow was Anna and Billy's thirteenth birthday. As of midnight, Billy was officially going to be cursed.

The bad weather doubled the danger for the male Grimsbanes.

"Can't be going outside today," muttered elderly Great-Uncle Monty as he stared out the front window. "Might not even be able to open the door."

Anna, who was already clad in a significant amount of face paint to look like an undead skater, grimaced uncomfortably as she handed him his afternoon coffee. "Uh, sorry to hear that."

"Taking a risk even looking out the window," he continued, as if Anna hadn't even spoken. "What if a bird were to crash through right now? Could kill me."

For one hideous second, as Anna stared at her wrinkled, cautious uncle who always sported a furrowed brow and pronounced scowl, she could see an echo of Billy's features written on his face. It was so jarring, she took a step back, nearly tripping over the sign with the names of all the dead people and their funeral times.

"Scuse me," Anna muttered, brushing past Great-Uncle Monty. She continued through the foyer and up a hallway, still perturbed by the sudden similarity between her relatives. The idea that Billy could end up like Great-Uncle Monty when he was older shook her to her core.

Over the last few days, Billy had become considerably withdrawn—locking himself in his bedroom and reading late into the night. Anna could hear him incessantly scribbling in the margins of his books. Lying in her bed with nothing but her thoughts and the Kurt Mackenzie poster on her ceiling, Anna couldn't help her mind from wandering to Billy's impending curse. The fear of him being in constant danger once the curse set in had kept Anna awake for several nights in a row.

Anna passed Madeline lying on the sitting room couch, texting on her phone.

As Anna walked by Madeline, she once again felt a tingling on the back of her neck—the same tingling she'd felt on the porch a few days ago. This time, it felt taller somehow, as if a vulture were watching her from a perch atop a tree.

Anna looked up, but the ceiling seemed as normal as ever.

"What are you doing?" Madeline asked.

Anna rubbed the back of her neck. "I don't know. I keep getting this weird feeling. Like I'm being watched."

Madeline scoffed. "Oh, so the Watcher's after you now?"

"No, I just—"

"You're just attention-seeking, again."

"I am *not* seeking attention."

"First the diary, now this?" Madeline shook her head. "You have *got* to get a hold of yourself."

"How many times do I have to tell you I'm not the one who took the diary?" Anna shouted. "I didn't steal it—honestly!"

All week, family members had been whispering behind their hands and exchanging knowing glances whenever Anna passed. Anna was certain Madeline and Camille weren't the only Grimsbanes who blamed her for the diary going missing. It was making her absolutely miserable.

"Whatever." Madeline went back to texting.

Anna glanced up at the ceiling. The feeling still hadn't subsided, but Madeline clearly wasn't sensing anything. Anna must have been imagining it. That was the only explanation.

Anna entered the main office, where Mom and Dad were fielding the significant number of calls that always seemed to increase with the Halloween holiday.

"No," said Dad into the funeral home phone as Anna walked in. "Yes, I'm very sorry to hear about your loss, Mr. Stine. We'll send someone over to get the body right away. No, I wouldn't touch him if I were you." Dad winced, rubbing the bridge of his nose as he grabbed his coffee from Anna. "Oh, you already have? Okay, don't worry. It won't impact anything, but you may want to wash your hands—"

"Why would you hunt a necromancer on Halloween?" Mom shouted into her cell phone, seated in one of the leather armchairs in front of Dad's desk. "Well, I'm sorry, Tom, but I'm not sending my relatives into a death trap just because you and your family were stupid enough to engage—" Mom held the phone away from her ear as the man on the other end began shouting, exchanging an eye roll with Anna as she took the coffee. "Thanks."

"Who's that?" Anna asked.

Mom placed her phone on mute. "Tom Jackson, head of Ohio's branch of the Knights of Van Tassel. Seems he and some of his kids decided to take on a witch last night. They're finishing the job in a few hours and want me to send some people down to help."

Anna furrowed her brow. "Why won't you?"

"Number one rule of hunting: engage, incapacitate, and kill. Number two rule of hunting: never, ever hunt on Halloween," explained Mom. "Like I said during the family meeting, on Halloween any area around a witch turns into a cryptid soup."

Anna wrinkled her nose. "Gross."

"Exactly. No one likes fighting cryptid soup." Mom scrunched her face at the shouting on the other end of the phone. "Except Tom, apparently."

Anna laughed.

The tingling feeling sharply subsided—so suddenly that Anna nearly gasped at the unexpected relief. It was as if the invisible vulture had taken flight—its attention now turned to a more suitable meal.

Mom furrowed her brow. "Everything okay?"

Anna nodded quickly. "Yeah. Yeah. I'm fine." She glanced up at the now empty-feeling ceiling. "Just jumpy."

"No reason to be jumpy," said Mom, smiling in her usual warm manner. "The most dangerous cryptids will stay far into the Not-So-Witchless Woods—close to the Watcher. Besides, cryptids tend to be wary of groups of humans, and you'll be with Billy, Suvi, and Rosario all night. There's absolutely nothing to worry about."

"Right," said Anna, nodding. The Grimsbanes had been raiding the Not-So-Witchless Woods for three hundred forty years. Despite this, they'd never been able to pin down the Watcher's exact location, though they knew she *had* to be somewhere near the center of the forest, where the most dangerous cryptids gathered every Halloween. No matter how close the Grimsbanes got to catching the Watcher, she managed to evade them at the last second—vanishing as if she'd never been there in the first place. She was never spotted close to town. There was no way the tingling feeling was the Watcher spying on *Anna*.

Anna began leaving the room.

"Remember to wear reflective tape!" Dad shouted after her.

"I will!" responded Anna, certain she'd rather have a car strike her dead than deal with the social humiliation that would come with wearing reflective tape.

Anna trotted up the stairs to the attic. "Billy!" she called, rapping on his door twice. She went to her room to gather everything she needed for the evening. "Billy, c'mon! We're gonna be late!" Anna grabbed her skateboard and pillowcase and crossed back to Billy's room. She opened Billy's door.

Billy was standing in front of her in his normal-person clothes: a cream sweater, lace-up boots, and dark green pants. His hair was combed, and he had used *waaaay* too much gel—so much so that his hair looked like it had been covered in a layer of clear paint.

"I can explain," said Billy, holding his hands up.

"What exactly are you supposed to be?" Anna asked.

"What?"

"We're all supposed to be dressed as zombies, and you're dressed like—" Anna gestured to him. "I dunno, an Irish sheep farmer or something!"

Billy blanched. He turned to look in the mirror. "Oh no!" He attempted to run his hand through his incredibly stiff hair, and it got stuck. "Oh God, I look like a sheep farmer!"

"Is that not what you were going for?"

"Why would I be going for *sheep farmer*? I was going for more of the daring adventurer type!"

"Since when have daring adventurers worn corduroy pants?"

"I need to get changed." Billy scrambled to his dresser.

Anna leaned against his door frame. "I hope you've got your own face paint, because I used all mine up."

"I'm not going trick-or-treating," Billy said, his back to her as he sifted through the drawer.

Anna blinked. "I'm sorry, what?"

"I'm not going trick-or-treating," Billy repeated, turning around. "With the curse and everything, I'm just not in the mood to go around begging for candy that I won't be able to eat in the morning when I develop a severe peanut and soy allergy."

"You're *not* going trick-or-treating?" Anna asked, not believing what she was hearing. "You're ditching us?"

"I'm not ditching you, per se," said Billy, pulling a pair of jeans out of his dresser. "I'm just—" He shrugged. "Having an alternate evening to yours."

Anna's mind whirred through the options of what

Billy's "alternate evening" might be, before landing on the only viable option. "Are you going to Xander's party?"

Billy paused. "I—uh—" He gulped.

"You *are* going to Xander's party, aren't you?" Anna stepped into his room, pointing a finger at him. "You're ditching us to hang out with a bunch of strangers!"

Billy took a deep breath. "Look, Anna, I just have some things I want to do before I get cursed and—"

"Billy, you'll have *plenty* of years to go to parties once I break the curse, but this may be our last time trick-or-treating! You can't just abandon us!"

"I get that you and Suvi and Rosario want to go trick-or-treating, but I'm just not interested," Billy said seriously. "Not tonight."

"I hope you're not going to try to convince me to join you," Anna said, rolling her eyes, "because there's no way *I'm* turning my back on Suvi and Rosario."

Billy looked down, rubbing the back of his neck. He closed his eyes and sighed deeply, just like he always did when he was wording something carefully. "I . . . kind of don't want you to come with me. I want to go alone."

A strange mixture of hurt and confusion twisted around Anna's heart as she processed what her brother had said. She and Billy did everything together.

Anna swallowed, trying to keep her voice steady. "What do you mean?"

Billy sighed. "You remember back at the family meeting? I was trying to convince the family to let me stay in school, and they were all yelling at me—a *whole room* full of people was yelling at me about something I *really* care about, and I looked at you for backup because we *always* back each other up, no questions asked, and you—" He scoffed. "Well, Anna, you just stared at me. You just—" Billy shook his head. "I just—"

"You don't think you can trust me?" Anna finished, understanding what Billy was saying.

Billy grimaced, then slowly, almost imperceptibly, he nodded.

Anna's heart fell to her shoes. "Billy, you know I couldn't back you up about the school thing. It's too dangerous. You *know* it's too dangerous."

"Regardless of your *personal opinion*," Billy continued, rolling his eyes, "you didn't help me when I needed you."

"Because I wanted to keep you safe!"

"I don't *need* you to keep me safe!" Billy shouted

in a sudden burst of emotion. "I'm just as capable as you are!"

Anna considered this. In all honesty, she didn't think Billy was as capable as she was. Sure, he had more book smarts than she did, but when it came to practical matters of life—brawn, people skills, street smarts—Anna was more equipped than her twin was. She wasn't about to tell him that, though.

"I know you can handle yourself, Billy," Anna lied, "but we're better as a team."

"I get that," Billy clarified. "It *is* okay if we do things on our own, though."

"On your own?" Anna echoed, the confusion and hurt subsiding as anger began to bubble up within her. "Without me?"

"Is that such a bad thing?" Billy shouted.

"Yes, it is a bad thing!" Anna yelled, anger that was rarely directed at Billy rushing in her chest. "You're leaving me behind! You're just like everyone else in the family! It's bad enough they're always leaving me out, but I never imagined you would too!"

Billy's jaw dropped, but he quickly righted himself. "Well, what about you?"

Anna recoiled. "What about me?"

"You think I'm helpless, just like the rest of the family does!" Billy yelled. "You think I'm so weak that I can't even go to school when the curse sets in—that I can't even go to a party *before* the curse sets in! That I'm not smart enough to take care of myself!"

"That's totally different!"

"You don't get it!" Billy shouted, throwing his hands up. "You just don't get it!"

Anna took a step back. "Fine, then." Anna thundered out of the room and stomped down the stairs. She couldn't *believe* Billy was acting this way. He was ditching her—leaving her in the dust like the hunters in the family always did.

"Wait, Anna!" called Billy, running to catch up with her.

She felt Billy's hand on her shoulder and was suddenly spun backward into a hug. Anna tensed, her anger morphing into confusion. She and Billy were close, but they never ever hugged. Hugging was awkward—something for prissy families that took Christmas card photos in matching pajamas—definitely not something for the rough-and-tumble Grimsbanes.

Anna wriggled out of the hug and took a step back. "What's your problem?"

"I want to tell you—" Billy took a deep breath. "I'm really sorry. For everything."

"Right," said Anna, taking another step back. "You kind of should be."

And with that, Anna marched off down the stairs, not bothering to look back.

6

Tricks and Treats

Anna skated down her driveway in a great huff. She and Billy almost never fought, and when they did, it was usually about stupid stuff like who was taking up more counter space in the bathroom. This argument, though, hit harder than any other. The one person Anna had always relied on—the only family member who always included her—had totally abandoned her. Every single Grimsbane had officially decided that Anna wasn't worthy of being included— that Anna wasn't wanted.

Luckily, Anna had two friends she could always rely on. Suvi and Rosario were waiting for her, and

Anna wasn't about to let Billy's mean comments ruin their Halloween.

"Hey, kid! Are you a Grimsbane?" asked a tourist as she passed the Grimsbane Family Funeral Home sign.

"I'm a zombie!" Anna pointed to her face paint as she skated away. "Obviously."

The tourist sneered. "Aren't you a little old to be trick-or-treating?"

"Probably!" Anna yelled, feeling her face grow hot. "Not that it's any of your business!"

Anna reached Rosario's porch, picked up her skateboard, and made her way to a staircase hidden behind a tapestry at the back of the restaurant. She stepped over a discarded action figure on the landing and knocked on Rosario's bedroom door. Anna could hear the eighties Halloween hits blasting from inside.

Without waiting for an answer, Anna opened the door. If possible, Rosario's bedroom had become even more stuffed since Anna had last been there, though it was difficult to tell with all the Christmas lights, neon posters featuring teen pop stars, Squishmallows, and crystals covering every surface.

Suvi and Rosario sang along with the song as they put the finishing touches on their makeup. Rosario was teasing her hair up, dressed as a zombie hiker.

Suvi was using a hairbrush as a microphone and was dressed as a sort of quasi zombie-fairy, complete with blood, guts, and glitter. Her costume was *covered* in reflective tape.

Anna threw her hands up in exasperation. "Why is it I'm the only one around here who can be ready on time?"

Rosario turned to her, smiling. She looked behind Anna and frowned. "Where's Billy?"

"Not coming." Anna sat down on the wooden floor next to Rosario's speaker, placing her skateboard beside her.

"Why not?" asked Suvi, turning around.

"He—" Anna paused. Even after the fight, Anna didn't want to cause Billy any trouble. She didn't want their friends to be mad at Billy. They'd be furious if they knew he'd ditched them to hang out with Xander.

"Billy's feeling a little down about the curse," said Anna. "He said he might catch up later."

"Oh," said Suvi quietly, looking back at the mirror.

A silence passed between the three of them. As Anna thought about it, she realized this would be their first time trick-or-treating without Billy. She recalled the memories their friend group had made throughout their childhood—dressing as superheroes and baseball players and, on one particularly odd year, each other. Billy had abandoned it all for a party—admittedly, a cool high school party that would probably be way more fun than trick-or-treating, but he'd abandoned them nonetheless.

Anna sat up and crossed her legs. "Do we have a game plan?"

Suvi nodded. "Obtain as many king-sized candy bars as possible. We'll start at Heatherbrae Court, then repeat the neighborhood, then go to Bloomington Heights."

"I think we should go to Bloomington Heights first," said Rosario. "There's more rich people there, so there will be more king-sized candy."

Anna was about to agree, but something made her hesitate. Billy had been acting so weird today, and, despite her anger, Anna was worried about him. This, coupled with the anxiety resulting from her relatives accusing her of stealing the diary and the weird watching feeling she kept getting, was weighing on Anna like a school bus. "Maybe we should try to get home early this year."

Suvi nodded sagely. "Because of the werewolf situation?"

"Huh?"

Suvi gestured out the window, where the last orange light of the sunset was fading into purple. "Full moon tonight."

Anna shook her head. "No. Billy's acting weird—like, really weird. He gave me a hug when I left."

"*Billy* gave you a hug?" asked Suvi.

"*Right?*"

"I don't necessarily think that's weird," answered Rosario, now examining one of her crystals intently. "He might just be upset about the curse. It's a big change for him—for all of us."

"Okay, well, he also said some really mean things," said Anna.

"Like what?" asked Suvi.

"Like, that I'm not trustworthy because I don't stick up for him and that he should do stuff on his own without me," Anna continued, crossing her arms.

Rosario wrinkled her nose, still staring intently at the crystal. "Emotions are running high. He didn't mean it. There's just a lot going on. That doesn't make it okay that he said what he said, but you've got to look at it from his perspective."

Anna scrunched up her face in displeasure. She had absolutely no desire to view things from Billy's perspective.

"We should get going," said Suvi, picking up her pillowcase. "The good candy'll be gone if we don't leave soon."

The second Suvi left the room, Rosario turned to Anna. "Is Billy actually staying in tonight, or did you make that up?"

Anna blinked. How had Rosario known she was lying?

"He's going to Xander's party," Anna answered.

Rosario took a deep, calming breath with her eyes closed, then another, then another. Anna rolled her eyes. Rosario very rarely got angry, but when she did, she always took deep breaths to compose herself before talking. Did this diffuse tensions? Yes. Did it take up an awful lot of time that Anna had very little patience for? Also yes.

Rosario opened her eyes, smiling at Anna. "Let's not let Billy's absence ruin our evening." With that, Rosario left the room, leaving Anna no choice but to follow.

The residents of Bloomington Heights didn't get suspicious until Anna, Suvi, and Rosario's third pass through the neighborhood.

"Haven't I given you candy already?" asked a bespectacled old woman resembling a Pomeranian, narrowing her eyes suspiciously.

"I don't think so," Rosario answered, holding out her pillowcase.

The woman's eyes narrowed farther. "Aren't you a bit old for trick-or-treating?"

"Actually," said Anna, "we're six and a half."

The woman's eyebrows shot up her forehead. "Six and a half?"

Anna nodded. "We're tall for our age."

Even after they left Bloomington Heights, Heatherbrae Court was good enough for two rounds before Anna, Suvi, and Rosario finally decided to go home. They struggled to carry their bulging pillowcases as they ambled down the street, already stuffed with candy to the point of bursting.

Anna considered it a pretty successful Halloween, even if her mind did keep drifting to Billy. Despite the fun of the night and the successful candy haul, it didn't feel right without him there.

As Anna, Suvi, and Rosario approached the warm, yellow glow of the windows of the Blue Moon, Anna heard a familiar voice behind them.

"Greetings and salutations!" called Xander, passing

them as he strode to the restaurant. He spun on his heel, facing the girls as he walked backward. "You guys missed a heck of a party. We ate, like, forty pizzas and played a mean game of Settlers of Catan, all while watching *Massacre at Blood Lake Seven: The Slayening.*"

Despite herself, Anna stood up a bit taller, a smirk crossing her face. Though Billy enjoyed pizza and nerdy board games, he'd nearly puked when he and Anna watched the sixth Blood Lake movie. He was not a blood-and-guts person. If they watched the newest Blood Lake movie at Xander's party, Billy must've had a terrible time. Served him right, after abandoning Anna and their friends.

"Have you got any Snickers?" Xander asked, pointing at Rosario's bag. "I'm, like, starving."

"I thought you were against trick-or-treating," Suvi said.

Xander rolled his eyes. "Just because I don't want to run around the neighborhood making a fool of myself doesn't mean I can't appreciate a good candy bar."

Anna shook her head. "That's not how it works. You and Billy didn't go trick-or-treating, so you and Billy don't get any candy."

Xander furrowed his brow. "What are you talking about, dude?"

"It's only fair," Rosario agreed. "You and Billy went to the party instead of putting in the work. You guys can't expect us to give you our candy."

"Nah, I get that," Xander said, waving her off. "It's just that Billy didn't go to the party."

Anna stopped in her tracks. She looked to Rosario, who seemed just as perplexed as Anna was.

"What do you mean, he didn't go to the party?" asked Suvi, her brow furrowed. "I thought Billy was staying home tonight."

"He *definitely* didn't stay home," said Xander. "I ran into Billy while I was walking to the party. I asked what he was doing—if he was planning on going with me, but he said he was going with you guys." Xander paused. "Well, he didn't say that exactly. He said he had something important to do."

"Where was he going?" Anna asked, her confusion beginning to morph into fear. Billy was going to be cursed in a few hours' time. If he hadn't gone trick-or-treating and he hadn't gone to Xander's party, then where was he?

"I'm not sure," said Xander. "All I know is that he was taking a shortcut through the forest."

7

Behind the Bookcase

Before Anna knew what she was doing, she was already halfway across the street, making her way to the Grimsbane Family Funeral Home, swimming through the sea of tourists who had gathered to take their picture by the funeral home's sign. Xander's statement bounced around Anna's head like a Ping-Pong ball, ringing through her skull a thousand times as she tried to process what he'd said. Billy wouldn't have gone into the forest—not *today*. Not on Halloween! Not with the curse setting in just a few hours from now! Going into the forest would kill him!

"Anna, wait!" called Suvi, running behind her.

"Xander, cover for us!" Rosario shouted over her shoulder as she approached Anna.

"You know I will, dude! You know I will!" Xander's voice was distant. "But you better save me some Snickers!"

Anna continued up the driveway, Suvi and Rosario close behind. "Something is seriously wrong! Billy knows how dangerous the forest is! We need to tell somebody! We need to—"

Anna felt Rosario's hand on her shoulder and stopped. She turned.

"Take a deep breath," Rosario said calmly, grabbing both of Anna's shoulders. *"Relax."*

"Are you *serious* right now?" Anna couldn't believe Rosario was suggesting deep-breathing exercises at a time like this.

Rosario took a deep breath. "Look, I know this is confusing, but Billy's really smart. He never makes decisions that are *this* bad."

Suvi nodded in agreement. "He might've been taking a small shortcut through the forest on the way to some other shindig—a little risky, but nothing that's totally out of order. We don't need to tell anyone yet."

"So what do you suggest we do?" asked Anna.

"We'll check out his room," Rosario said. "See if he left any notes about where he was going, which, knowing Billy, he definitely did."

Anna considered this. Billy had always been a sticky-note kind of person. If he was going anywhere, or making any sort of plan, he would've written it on a colorful sticky note and put it somewhere. Even so, Anna didn't like the idea of delaying. The Not-So-Witchless Woods was crawling with cryptids, and, if Billy was in the forest, he could be in serious danger. However, despite their fight, Anna didn't want to get Billy in trouble if it wasn't necessary. She still wanted to protect him.

"Fine," Anna said, "we'll check out his room before we tell anyone, but we need to hurry."

She, Suvi, and Rosario tromped up the damp steps of the funeral home, their shoes squeaking on the wet cheerleading mats lining the porch. Upon opening the front door, Anna wasn't surprised to see everything even quieter than usual. On Halloween, the Grimsbane women made patrols about the town, in case any cryptid managed to sneak past the bounds of the forest. By now, most of the men would be in bed, or otherwise engaging in some kind of safe, quiet activity.

Together, Anna, Suvi, and Rosario made their way to the attic.

Billy's room looked just as it had this afternoon. His bed was still made in its usual tidy fashion. Posters from nerdy books and movies still lined the walls. His books were still stacked in neat, alphabetized rows on his bookshelf. There was no obvious indication that anything was amiss.

Anna paused, looking at the room, trying to take deep breaths like Rosario did. Logical. She had to be logical like Billy.

Suvi crossed to Billy's desk and examined his sticky notes, pulling them off the wall. *Math: page 137, problems 1–8.* Suvi tossed a pink sticky note over her shoulder. *Monsters and Mayhem: 6 pm, Thursday.* She tossed that note and two more. "This all seems like pretty standard stuff."

Rosario sighed, crossing to help. "Maybe you're missing something. Is anything written on the back?"

Anna paused, looking around the room. If she wanted to figure out why Billy had gone into the forest, Anna would have to look at things as Billy would. What vibe had he been going for with this evening's outfit? The daring adventurer type? Just like the heroes from his stories.

Stories.

Anna turned to face the bookshelf. It stored the tales of all the heroes Billy admired. It was where he put his most prized possessions. If Billy was hiding secrets, he would undoubtedly try to involve his books.

Anna crossed the room. She grabbed the edge of the bookcase with both hands, took a deep breath, and pulled. The bookcase barely moved an inch.

Something clattered against the floor. Suvi and Rosario turned to look at Anna.

"What was that?" asked Rosario.

Anna peered into the space behind the bookshelf, squinting as she examined the wooden objects that had been wedged behind it. "There's something back here."

Anna picked one of the items up. A wooden tomahawk—a practice weapon taken from the storage room. She picked up a wooden axe and a plastic throwing knife.

Suvi's eyes widened. "Are those—"

"Practice weapons," Anna finished definitively, flipping the knife over in her hand dexterously.

Rosario had gone remarkably pale. "Has Billy . . . been *training* with practice weapons?"

"I'm not sure," Anna answered, examining the knife.

There would be absolutely no reason for Billy to be training with weapons, yet here they were, hidden in his bedroom. As such, he *had* to have been training with them . . . but why?

Anna turned to the space between the bookshelf and the wall, peering at the back of it. There was something written on it. She grabbed the side of the bookshelf. "Guys, help me with this."

Slowly, Anna, Suvi, and Rosario guided the bookcase across the floor. All the while, the light from Billy's single lamp further illuminated the writing on the back, revealing hastily scrawled words and shapes.

Anna stepped into the space between the shelf and the wall so she could properly see. Upon fully viewing Billy's masterpiece, her jaw dropped.

It wasn't just writing on the back of the bookcase. It was a map.

"It's Witchless," Rosario whispered.

Rosario was right. Billy had drawn everything from the funeral home to the Blue Moon to the Not-So-Witchless Woods surrounding the town in black Sharpie. Notes in his scrawled handwriting peppered the forest. Anna examined the note closest to her and saw that he had written *Page 70—Louisa Grimsbane, 1807—sighting of ghost—October 31.*

The one beside it read *Page 293—Dotty Grimsbane, 1938—sighting of the Jersey Devil—October 31.*

Sticky notes and drawings were littered among the sightings. The sticky notes included lists of weapons and strategies, such as *salt, lavender, iron needed*; *do not approach a White Screamer*; and *you're probably dead if you see a White Screamer, tbh.*

Anna stared at the notes for a minute, wondering why Billy was cataloging so much information about hunting.

It was then that Anna saw a bright blue sticky note in the middle of the map:

1684–present—The Watcher—October 31—ENGAGE, INCAPACITATE, KILL.

Here, Billy had drawn a giant red *X* and circled it.

Anna furrowed her brow, staring at the red *X*.

She took a step back and staggered on an uneven surface, nearly falling over. She glanced down and realized she'd been standing on a thick, leather-bound journal. Billy must have wedged it behind the bookcase.

A Guide to Hunting Witches, Monsters, and Spookes Moste Foul by Diligence Grimsbane and Descendants was written across the front in elegant, cursive script. Below that, someone else had written *Engage, Incapacitate, Kill.*

"No way," Anna muttered, a sudden flurry of emotions roiling through her as she picked up the journal. *Billy* had taken Diligence's diary? He'd let everyone blame her for stealing it all week! Why did he steal it in the first place?

"What is that?" Suvi asked.

"It's our family's journal—Diligence's diary," Anna answered, opening it. The familiar smell of old parchment tickled her nose as she flipped through the pages. It was almost illegible. Piles of notes crowded the margins, all signed with a year and a name. The actual text was written in black ink in different hands, always signed with the name of a Grimsbane woman. "It holds the entire family history—notes about every witch and cryptid we've ever fought, and every supernatural encounter we've ever had."

"Look, there's a page missing!" said Rosario, pointing down.

Anna would've missed it had Rosario not pointed it out. Billy had torn a page out of the diary. Where it had been, there was a barely visible bit of ripped edges.

Anna tried to make sense of everything. Billy was secretly researching witch hunting and had been extra careful to keep his research, as well as a map he had made of the Not-So-Witchless Woods, hidden from the family. Diligence's diary, the most important book in their family library, was in Billy's room. He'd let everyone believe Anna had stolen the diary, even though he was clearly the actual thief—

Anna gasped, staring in horror at the map and the giant red *X* in the middle of the forest, realizing what all this meant.

Billy—nerd extraordinaire, lover of scones, and soon-to-be walking death trap—had decided to hunt the Watcher, alone, on the most dangerous night of the year.

Billy was definitely going to die.

8

Into the Forest

Four Hours and Thirty Minutes Until Midnight

This," said Suvi seriously, a grin spreading across her face, "is going to be the best *Ghouligans* episode *ever*."

"Suvi!" Anna protested, closing the diary and turning to her friend. "This is *serious*. Billy's in real trouble. He's in the forest hunting the *Watcher*. Plus, it's Halloween, so the forest is full of cryptids—not to mention the Watcher herself, *and* he's getting cursed at midnight!"

Rosario was taking several extremely deep breaths. "Everything"—she took a breath—"will be"—she took a breath—"okay."

Anna racked her brain, trying to think of a plan.

She knew she should tell her family, but the hunters were scattered throughout town. By the time she informed everyone, all the women returned, and Anna explained the situation, Billy could be even farther into the forest than he was now. It would be even closer to midnight. Billy would be in more danger than ever.

"It's up to us," Anna said quietly.

"I'm sorry, what?" asked Rosario, stopping her deep breaths.

"It's up to us," Anna repeated. "Billy's out in the forest looking for the Watcher. If midnight hits, he's as good as dead. We need to find him before the witch or something else kills him. *We* have to save Billy."

"I can't really say I agree," said Rosario. She walked to Billy's bed and sat cross-legged on it. "For one thing, our parents are going to realize we snuck out."

"Xander already said he'd cover for us in exchange for Snickers," said Anna. "He'll probably tell Suvi's mom and my parents we're sleeping over your house, and will tell your moms you're sleeping over my house."

"Fair enough," muttered Rosario, "but Billy isn't an experienced hunter. It's very likely he'll tire himself out and come home."

Anna shook her head. "You *know* Billy. He's a total

klutz, with or without the curse. He could've sprained his ankle or fallen or—"

"Be dead in a ditch somewhere," said Suvi matter-of-factly, plopping onto the floor.

"Well, yeah, that too," said Anna quietly, trying to get that image out of her mind.

"How do you know the Watcher will even go after him?" asked Rosario. "I thought you said she was nearly impossible to hunt."

Anna grimaced at that, remembering the strange feeling that had come and gone over the past few days—like someone was constantly looking down at her, or over her shoulder, or directly at the back of her neck.

"I don't think the Watcher will go after him, exactly," Anna admitted, "but I do think that she's taken up more interest in the family than usual."

Rosario and Suvi exchanged a confused glance.

"What exactly . . . do you mean?" asked Rosario.

Anna took a deep breath, then quickly explained the watching feeling she'd experienced.

"Wait a minute," said Suvi, shaking her head in confusion. "There's a witch stalking you, and you didn't tell your parents?"

"Well, Madeline said I was seeking attention, and I

didn't want to prove her right, and no one else felt it, so I assumed I was imagining things."

Suvi, who was an only child, still seemed a bit confused, but Rosario, who had several older siblings, nodded sagely in understanding.

"Okay," said Rosario calmly. "The witch is watching you. Do you think she's watching Billy, too?"

"I don't know," Anna answered, "but regardless, we still need to go look for him."

Anna stood up, took a red marker off Billy's desk, and circled the location of the Watcher.

"Billy's going to be heading toward the center of the forest, where the Watcher is, so we also have a secondary mission. We need to hunt the Watcher, kill her, and break the family curse."

"Don't you think killing seems a bit unnecessary?" asked Rosario, scrunching her face in displeasure. "If—and that's a big if—we go after Billy, what does that have to do with the witch? This is a rescue mission, not a hunt."

"Killing the witch is definitely necessary. When I talk about witches, I'm not talking about your average blue-haired lady with herbs and mason jars. I'm talking about cold-blooded, black-eyed monsters whose hobbies include experimenting on animals, hexing innocent people, and eating children. Their souls are so corrupted a single match can set them alight, so yeah, killing's gonna be necessary. If she's in the forest, she's a danger to us, and a danger to Billy. Besides, if we break the curse *before* midnight, then Billy won't get cursed *at* midnight. Therefore, killing the witch, and breaking the curse as a result, is a really important part of the rescue mission. If Billy isn't cursed, then it'll be much easier to get him home safely."

Anna didn't mention that she'd wanted to hunt the Watcher her whole life—that though she was incredibly worried about Billy, this was the perfect opportunity for her to hunt the witch. This was Anna's chance to show everyone who doubted her that she was more than they thought she was—that she *deserved* to be a hunter. For a moment, Anna imagined the look on Madeline's face if Anna were the one to kill the Watcher, the apologies from family members for not letting her hunt earlier; even Billy saying sorry for not including Anna in *his* witch hunt.

Anna continued, "You guys don't have to worry about the actual killing part, though." She capped the marker. "I'll handle that."

Rosario sighed, crossing her arms as she stared at the mess surrounding them, her brow furrowed.

"Anna, I know you're scared about Billy—we all are. We have to be reasonable, though. You have no hunting experience."

Anna wrinkled her nose. There it was again—the same doubt that everyone had in her. "I'm a Grimsbane, Rosario. Hunting's in my blood. I know so much about hunting that I'm basically already a witch hunter. I don't really have a choice, either. Billy could be hurt, and if the Watcher finds him—"

"You should call your mom," Rosario said. "We shouldn't be trying to kill anybody."

"There's no *time* to call her. She'd tell me to stay put and I'd have to listen, but the women in my family are too scattered about the town, and the men are too cursed to do anything helpful. By the time they come up with a plan, it'll be too late. We only have until midnight to find Billy. We need to go *now*, and I'm going with or without you."

"Same," said Suvi, nodding in agreement. "We're the only chance Billy has at making it home safely. Also, I think it'd be cool to see a witch in real life."

Rosario leaned back against Billy's bed frame like a business executive sitting in a dull meeting. "You're going to get yourselves killed."

"Do you have a better suggestion?" asked Suvi. "It

seems like ghost hunting's the best option."

"Witch hunting," corrected Anna.

"Same difference."

Anna and Suvi stared determinedly at Rosario, who was now staring straight at them with a resolutely skeptical expression, waiting for one of them to cave. Anna knew it would take more than a witch and her missing brother to convince Rosario to join such a violence-heavy cause. Whether Anna liked it or not, she'd have to compromise.

"Look at it this way," said Anna. "All we're *really* trying to do is find Billy. If we do find him, we'll come back home without seeing the Watcher at all. If we do come across the Watcher or any other cryptid, I'm not asking you to kill them. That's my job. You're more than welcome to try to negotiate. When that fails, I'll take charge and handle the actual hunting part. If you don't go, I'll have no choice but to go full-hunter mode." Anna shrugged. "Your choice."

Rosario narrowed her gaze at Anna and pursed her lips. For a moment, Anna thought she wasn't convinced.

Rosario sighed. "Fine. I'll go—"

"YES!" shrieked Suvi.

"I'll go," continued Rosario, "but only to find Billy

and handle everything as peacefully as possible, and you have to promise you won't resort to violence unless absolutely necessary."

"Sure," said Anna, smiling. "I promise. Now, let's come up with a game plan."

Anna, Suvi, and Rosario split up and went to their separate homes to gather what they could for the witch hunt. Anna collected her supplies quietly so as to not disturb the Grimsbane men. Knowing she, Suvi, and Rosario would need food, Anna dumped her school supplies out of her red backpack and filled it with candy. She grabbed a custom-made, iron-infused golf club from her older cousin's golf bag (all supernatural creatures *hated* iron), the last bottle of lavender water from the storeroom (ghosts *really* hated lavender), a flashlight, and Diligence's diary, just in case they needed to quickly reference something while on the hunt.

Lastly, Anna grabbed the three essential things for witch killing: salt, to trap the witch; kindling, to help the fire along; and finally, a lighter. She wished she had access to the flamethrowers and salt-covered iron lassos in the basement, but the door was always locked when the women weren't home.

Anna stepped into the cool night, rubbing the last of her makeup off on the sleeve of her thick, camouflage coat. Leaves skittered around her hand-me-down sneakers as she crossed the abandoned street to Suvi's house.

Rosario stood on Suvi's front porch, now sporting a pink puffer coat with a fur-lined hood and turning a flashlight over in her hand.

"You didn't want anything else to defend yourself?" whispered Anna as she approached.

"I'm perfectly prepared," Rosario said.

Anna rolled her eyes. Leave it to Rosario to roll up to a haunted forest on the most haunted night of the year with nothing useful. "At least take my lavender water."

"What would I need lavender water for?"

"Uh, to burn a ghost that's trying to possess you?" said Anna. "It's Halloween! We don't know what's in that forest!"

"I don't think ghosts would do that sort of thing unless they were provoked."

"Ghosts do that sort of thing all the time! My cousin Camille—oh God, what are you wearing?"

Suvi had just emerged from her house looking very much like a one-man band. She wore an apparatus that gave the impression she'd been skewered by a number of swords, most of which were concentrated near her head.

"Backpack's full of candy and has a camera on it," explained Suvi, turning so Anna and Rosario could see. "There's a front-facing camera on the vest. The helmet's got a back-facing and front-facing camera, in addition to a few GoPros that'll show my facial expressions."

Anna sighed deeply. *"Why?"*

"Ghouligans," said Suvi triumphantly as she turned on her iPad's camera. "If we find the Watcher, great. If we can get video evidence that there's actually a witch in this forest, even better. It would really help me gain a following on YouTube."

"We aren't here to get *evidence*, though," said Anna. "What if it upsets the Watcher?"

Suvi snorted. "What's she gonna do? Kill us?"

"Maybe! She might! She killed Perseverance Grimsbane!"

"I don't think anyone kills unless they have to," said Rosario.

"Serial killers do," said Suvi pointedly. She paused, turning nervously toward Anna. "You don't—" She coughed. "You don't think there's any of *them* in the woods, do you?"

"Yep. Worst part is they look like everyone else, so we'd never know if we saw one."

"Don't tease her, Anna. She'll get freaked out," scolded Rosario.

Suvi sputtered. "I'm not gonna freak out."

"Then let's get a move on," said Anna, shoving the lavender water into Rosario's hands and then zipping up her own backpack. She set off in the direction of the forest, her friends closely following behind.

Anna checked the watch on her wrist. Just four hours until midnight. Four hours until she and Billy turned thirteen, and Billy was as good as dead.

She was determined to save her brother, and she wasn't going to let a forest full of cryptids stand in her way.

9

Almost a Deer

Three Hours and Thirty Minutes until Midnight

An update to the Ghouligans," said Suvi, speaking directly into the camera dangling above her head like the light of an angler fish. "We've been walking for thirty minutes. No sign of witches, but we're facing other horrors here in the Not-So-Witchless Woods. For one thing, the satellite signal clunked out about twenty minutes ago. For another, Rosario ate all the Kit Kats—"

"That was Anna."

"Was not," Anna called over her shoulder. "I've been eating candy corn."

"Who in their right mind eats *candy corn*?"

"People who are concerned about the dwindling number of Kit Kats."

"Excuse me," interrupted Suvi. "Some of us are trying to make a *video*."

Anna huffed, continuing to lead her friends farther into the forest. Suvi's monologue faded into the back of her mind as she stepped over a gnarled tree root.

The Not-So-Witchless Woods was a particularly dreary place during the day, but it was much worse at night. The second Anna entered the forest, she couldn't shake the strange, tingling feeling that she was being watched. The leaf-strewn path slunk around the trees in a looping pattern that had a tendency to wander and double back on itself—nearly impossible to see, let alone follow. The branches of the thick-trunked trees swayed and bent in the breeze. The leaves whispered and rustled as if gossiping about the scene below them. The full moon was just barely visible between the branches, like a great eye watching Anna, Suvi, and Rosario from above. This, coupled with the fact there could have been a murderous witch or bloodthirsty cryptid lurking in any of the hundreds of silently shifting shadows, meant the forest was a particularly unpleasant place to be on Halloween night.

Anna slid Diligence's diary out of her backpack

and pointed her flashlight at it, hoping to distract herself from the eeriness of the forest, still keeping an ear out for Billy. She scanned the table of contents, which detailed all manner of cryptids, witches, and hunts her family had been on.

She noted that Billy had torn out the page relating to secret societies. Anna couldn't remember ever reading that page when she'd snuck a peak at Diligence's diary. She'd been more interested in information relating to the Watcher. Now she was seriously regretting that decision. Billy must've found something on that page that would help with his hunt—something that was leading him deeper into the forest.

Anna, trying to get as much information about the Not-So-Witchless Woods and the Watcher as possible, turned to Diligence's entry on Halloween and began to read.

> The moste foule gathering of spirits
> occurrs on All Hallows' Eve. Spirits
> and spookes, drawn by the power
> of the Watcher, invade the forest,
> recking much havock. On this day,
> Grimsbanes must nott hunt in the
> wood, as the spookes who gather

are sertainly at their moste powerful and are given to flights of fancy that make them particullarly mallicious. The circle of cryptids and spirits surrounds the Watcher, tho she vanishes before all who try to hunt her, making the hunt useless. We have long sot a material to draw the witch out to no avail, but—

"Did you hear that?" Rosario whispered.

"Hear what?" asked Anna, turning to face her.

Rosario held up a hand. "Listen."

Anna closed her eyes and listened to the sounds of the forest. A slight breeze rustled the leaves. An animal scurried through the underbrush, and—

Don't you laugh when the hearse goes by
'Cause you might be the next to die.

Anna froze. The singing was so quiet, she wouldn't have noticed it if Rosario hadn't pointed it out. The song sounded like a nursery rhyme—a soft, tinkling melody just barely whispered from every direction, as if the forest itself were singing it.

The worms crawl in, the worms crawl out,
Into your stomach, and out your
mouth.
They eat your intestines, they
scramble your heart.
Then you feel like you're falling
apart.

Anna heard a soft step on the path behind her and spun, expecting to see Billy. She recoiled in surprise.

There, silhouetted upon the moonlit path, just barely fifteen feet away from her, was a deer. It stared directly at the ground, with its head nearly between its legs, its large, impressive antlers almost touching the forest floor.

The animal was incredibly, impossibly still.

"Is it—" Suvi looked around her iPad at the deer. "Is it sick?"

The singing stopped.

Without looking up, the deer raised its front hoof and took a step forward. It staggered and took another. Then another. Then another. The deer's movements were slow and jerky, as if it were an automaton rather than an animal, with joints made of brass rather than bone, lurching forward like clockwork. With every step, the deer's breath grew more ragged.

Moving slowly, as to not startle the animal, Anna reached to remove the golf club from her bag. She could feel her heart pounding against her chest. She tried to keep her breathing slow and even.

Anna's hand closed around the grip.

The deer looked up. Suvi screamed. Anna swung her club forward. Rosario grabbed Anna's arm and attempted to pull her back.

The deer's eyes were shining white, like two LED light bulbs had been forced into its skull. Its mouth pulled back in an unnatural way, creeping across its face in a sick smile, revealing rows and rows of pointed, canine teeth.

Anna's mind raced. This wasn't a deer. She'd read about this sort of cryptid—evil tricksters, servants of witches who roamed forests looking for people they could prey on.

This was a Not-Deer.

The Not-Deer's mouth wrenched open, then closed, then open again.

"Hello," the Not-Deer growled in a low, hollow voice, like it was speaking with lungs made of oil drums. "You know she can see you, right?"

The Not-Deer lurched forward.

Anna hurried backward, Rosario and Suvi beside her, not daring to look away from the Not-Deer. She swung the golf club in a wide arc, attempting to drive the cryptid back, but it continued on.

"She sees your brother, too, little hunter," the Not-Deer rasped. "I'm afraid you don't have much time to find him. He's getting boring, and she *hates* when people get boring. You, on the other hand—" The Not-Deer let out a human chuckle. "You've chosen such *interesting* companions. How fascinating to choose those you cannot trust—those with hidden agendas, those who keep secrets. It almost makes me want to smile."

The Not-Deer stopped, cracked its head sideways with a sickening CRUNCH, and continued forward.

Its smile began to stretch. The grin reached up its cheeks, until it was so wide that it revealed its back teeth and parts of its skull. The smile reached the ears atop its head, and the Not-Deer paused.

"I think you will be very entertaining," said the Not-Deer. Its head turned quizzically to the other side—slowly and impossibly, bones snapping and crunching under the strain, until its head was nearly upside down. "Don't you?"

A beam of light arched through the forest, casting the Not-Deer in shadow.

Someone grabbed Anna and pulled her roughly to the side of the path. They yanked her downward. She hit the ground behind a halfway-rotted log with a dull thump.

Muttering a curse, Anna quickly looked over the log.

The forest was empty, aside from the lights. The Not-Deer was gone—disappeared, as if it were made of smoke.

Anna breathed a sigh of relief and slumped back against the ground, clutching her beating chest with a shaking hand. She'd landed on her stomach, and her ribs were aching, but none of that seemed important. Not-Deer weren't necessarily deadly, but they were terrifying. They took great joy in psychologically torturing travelers. If one of them was around, it certainly didn't bode well for Billy or the girls.

"What was that thing?" Suvi whispered, staring at Anna with wide eyes.

"I think—" Anna gulped. "I think that was a Not-Deer. One of the Watcher's servants."

"*Quiet,*" Rosario whispered, pointing over the log. "There's people."

"*People?*" Anna looked back over the log.

Sure enough, three figures in dark purple cloaks were slowly making their way through the forest in single file. Their hoods were pulled so low, Anna couldn't see their faces. The first one in line had a flashlight pointed at a map.

Anna scoffed. *Tourists.* It didn't matter how many warnings the Grimsbanes gave throughout the Halloween season. Some visitors always tried to sneak into the forest to do some weird trend they'd found on TikTok or YouTube. These people must've managed to slip past the Grimsbane women's patrols of town.

Anna knew the protocol. She was supposed to escort the tourists back to Witchless, maybe offer a few photos "with a real, live Grimsbane!" and admonish them for their stupid decision. However, that just wasn't possible. Midnight was approaching quickly, and Anna had to prioritize rescuing Billy.

"Okay," whispered Anna, turning between Suvi and Rosario. "We've got to sneak away from the tourists. On my signal, we belly crawl through the forest until we find an alternative path. Ready, set—"

"Hang on," whispered Suvi, raising her iPad up.

Anna rolled her eyes. "Suvi, this is a *rescue mission*. We don't have time to film every little thing, especially with the Watcher tracking Billy."

"Just one minute," Suvi said, pressing the record button.

Anna turned to Rosario for support.

Rosario sighed. "Honestly, Anna, it'll be easier to get away if we wait for them to pass by. Then we don't have to worry about getting caught. Plus, we need some time to figure out what to do after what just happened with the Not-Deer."

Anna huffed, but she had to admit Rosario's plan made more sense than her own. She crouched lower behind the log, resigned to waiting.

"Are we there yet?" whined the third figure in line. Anna furrowed her brow. That man's voice sounded strangely familiar, though she couldn't put her finger on it.

"Does it *look* like we're there yet?" asked the figure in the front in a high, feminine voice.

"I don't know!" the third figure yelled, gesturing wildly with his robed arms. "We've been walking for ages!"

The figure in the middle sighed. "I *said* we should stop and ask the Mothman for directions."

The Mothman? Anna looked upward, expecting to see the red-eyed, winged figure perched in the trees above them, but all she could see was the moon peeking between the branches.

"The Mothman's an idiot!" the front figure shouted.

"He doesn't know the difference between the moon and a bug zapper!"

"He might not be the brightest bug-man on the planet," said the third, "but you have to admit he's great at parties. Do you remember the Alcatraz Grand Ritual in nineteen? With the karaoke machine? I've never heard someone sing 'Crazy Train' with so much passion!"

"His passion certainly didn't make up for his poor pitch!" The first one stopped in her tracks. "Well, that doesn't—" She turned the map upside down, then right side up. "Have we passed by here before?"

"At this rate we'll never get there on time!" called the middle. "You have to admit we're lost!"

"We aren't *lost*. We're just a bit turned around, that's all."

"I'm not being late *again* just because *you* were too proud to ask for directions!"

He lunged for the map in the first person's hands, but she quickly snatched it away. "In case you're forgetting, *I'm* the leader. As such, *I'm* the one who gets to hold the map."

"Just let me see it!" he shouted. "We can't miss the Grand Ritual!"

The figures began to squabble with one another, all grasping for the map.

"Grand Ritual?" Rosario whispered, looking to Anna and Suvi. "What's that?"

Suvi shrugged. "Never heard of it."

"Probably some internet thing they're trying out." Anna rolled her eyes. "You know how tourists are."

"THAT IS TOTALLY OUT OF ORDER!" screamed the first person in line, knocking the hood off the third person.

The man stood up, and Anna stifled a scream. She knew that person. She saw that person every time she went in her bedroom. She saw him first thing in the morning and right before she went to bed at night. He'd been the highlight of her and Rosario's sleepovers for the last two years. He was the star of the best movie series ever made!

That was Kurt Mackenzie—the star of *Vampires of West Grove High*.

10

The Order of the Third Eye

Three Hours Until Midnight

It took everything in Anna to keep from shouting out loud. That was Kurt Mackenzie! Anna turned to Rosario, who was silently screaming, tears brimming her eyes. They grabbed hands and turned back to the scene.

"I'm gonna throw up," Rosario whispered, wiping her tears away.

"*Me too!*" Anna grabbed Rosario's hand tighter.

Anna looked back to the figures, then shook her head and blinked, the initial excitement taking an abrupt back seat to the more pressing issue.

What on earth was Kurt Mackenzie doing in the Not-So-Witchless Woods?

"Hey!" Kurt shouted. He reached forward and knocked the hood off the first person. Anna braced herself.

The hood fell, and Anna let out a huff of disappointment. It was some random woman she'd never seen before. Unfortunately, she was not one of Kurt's costars.

Suvi gasped. She gestured nonsensically from the woman to Anna and Rosario with increasing wildness.

"What?" asked Anna.

"That lady's a famous chef," answered Suvi. "My dad collected all of her cookbooks! She has a show on TV!" Suvi zoomed in with her iPad.

"Hand the map here!" the second figure shouted. "I demand you give it here this instant!"

It was then that the second figure's hood fell. Anna's jaw dropped to the ground.

"Is that the president?" Suvi hissed.

"I don't know," Rosario whispered, blinking rapidly. "I still can't really see, because I'm crying, and Kurt Mackenzie is *here*—"

"That *is* the president," responded Anna. Anna had seen this guy a million times on the news, in magazines—his picture was even framed at the front of her history classroom, and here he was in the Not-So-Witchless Woods, squabbling over a map with Kurt Mackenzie and a chef.

"Listen here, Mr. President," said Kurt Mackenzie, now holding the map far above the others' heads. "I may be one of the youngest members of the Order, but I know my way around a forest. I had to do survival training for *Vampires of West Grove High Three*."

Anna perked up at the mention of the word "order." Could he possibly be talking about a secret society? She leaned in closer, trying to hear a bit better—to catch any hint of why Billy found the information about secret societies, and, potentially, this "Order," important enough to rip a page from Diligence's diary.

"And who was it that helped you get the contract to star in that teenybopper franchise?" asked the chef. She leapt into the air and grabbed the map from Kurt. "Me, that's who! I pulled every string I had at the studio!"

"And who was it that helped you get your first cookbook deal?" asked the president, snatching the map from the chef. "I was the one who called in the favor from the publishing house!"

"And who was it that *actually* went onstage during your debates?" asked Kurt, jabbing a finger at the president. "Do you know how hard it is to play *you* on live television?"

"It couldn't be *that* hard."

"I had stay in character for hours in *layers* of stage makeup!"

"*Quiet,*" hissed the chef. She and the president looked around nervously. "You shouldn't be making that much noise. We all know what happened in the sixties? When the Watcher caught Nixon?"

The whole group shuddered.

"Tore the third eye right out of his head," said the president.

Kurt hung his head despondently. "He never saw Watergate coming."

"My father was there to watch her catch him, you know," said the president. "Part of the reason I voted *against* returning to the Not-So-Witchless Woods for the Grand Ritual. Too risky with the Watcher and some of the more dangerous cryptids running about."

"Well, there are only so many magic-attuned places that can host a ritual of this magnitude!" said the chef.

"What about the Pine Barrens?" asked the president.

"The Seven Society booked the Pine Barrens a year in advance!"

"What about the Stanley Hotel?"

"Pretty sure the Bohemian Club got that," answered Kurt.

The three of them spit on the ground.

"Curse the Bohemian Club," said the chef.

"I still don't understand why we had to pick the Not-So-Witchless Woods," complained the president, putting his hands on his hips.

"Because the Watcher is a highly magical being," explained the chef, "and we need all the magical energy we can get if we want to summon ghosts."

A chill of fear rushed through Anna's heart. Ghosts, Anna knew, were dangerous and deadly. It didn't matter who they'd been in their previous life. They could possess, haunt, manifest, and murder. She had no idea how these people planned on summoning a ghost, but if they somehow managed to do so, that could cause some major problems.

"You seem to be ignoring the fact the Watcher can very well be stalking us at this instant," admonished the president.

"We don't *really* have to worry about the Watcher," interjected Kurt Mackenzie, waving the president off. "If we go invisible, there's no way she can track us."

Go invisible? Anna knew of only one magical

being who could go invisible—who had been going invisible for decades, thwarting the Grimsbanes' most important hunt: the Watcher. Whenever her family got even remotely close to her, the Watcher would totally disappear from view. Did the Order somehow know how the Watcher managed to disappear? Was that why Billy was interested in the Order?

"Now, let's see here." The president leaned in to look at the map. He looked up at the forest, then back down. "Oh, we are well and truly lost, aren't we?"

"I think desperate times call for desperate measures," said the chef.

"We're using the eye?" asked Kurt, a hint of excitement in his voice.

"I see no other option," said the chef. "Gentleman, let's gather hands."

Anna watched in confusion as the three figures joined together in a circle. They each took a deep breath, then turned their gazes skyward. They began muttering in a language Anna didn't understand, the same phrase over and over and over again, *"Video, ergo sum. Video, ergo sum."*

The president and Kurt continued chanting, while the chef spoke, "We members of the Order of the Third Eye compel the powers of the universe to open our gaze to the mysteries that surround us—to channel the magic of the forest, the magic of the witch known as the Watcher. *Video, ergo sum.*"

A great flash of purple light enveloped the forest. Anna squinted, using a hand to cover her eyes. As she blinked the light out of her vision, she looked back to the figures and gasped.

They each had a mega zit at the center of their forehead, easily the size of a golf ball. The zits bubbled and boiled and stretched, as if something was trying to reach out. Ripping and tearing noises echoed through the forest, along with grunts of pain from the three individuals, as glowing, purple eyes emerged right in the middle of their foreheads.

"Gross," whispered Rosario, wincing.

"Wicked," muttered Suvi, leaning forward to get a better view.

Anna felt a deep, instinctual growl escape the back of her throat. These people were dabbling in magic. They weren't witches, per se, but they were meddling with forces they shouldn't have been. They were putting themselves and everyone else in danger.

Looking at Kurt Mackenzie, and the glowing eye in his forehead, Anna felt her stomach lurch. She didn't know how much more disappointment and betrayal she could take tonight: first Billy, now Kurt.

"Ah, there's the path," said the chef. The three of them turned in unison to face the direction Anna knew went far deeper into the forest. "Clear as the eye on my forehead."

"I see it too," said Kurt, stretching. "We better get a move on. The ghosts won't summon themselves."

They began walking toward the center of the forest, slowly gliding just as they had before.

"Excuse me, Mr. President, sir!" Suvi shouted.

Anna clamped her hand over Suvi's mouth just as the peoples' heads snapped in their direction. Anna ducked and pulled Suvi down, hitting the ground. They were done for. Members of secret societies likely didn't take kindly to children spying on them, especially after eyes had just crawled their way out of their foreheads!

Anna took a deep breath and tightened her grip on the golf club. Slowly, silently, she stuck her head over the log.

To her relief, the people weren't looking at them. They were turning about the clearing, their eyes wide with fear.

"Hello?" Kurt shouted.

"Who's there?" yelled the chef.

Anna stayed silent, desperately hoping they didn't decide to investigate.

"Who's there?" the president shouted, panic barely audible behind his echoing voice.

"We need to get out of here," said the chef. She threw her hood back over her head. "Everyone, follow me."

Kurt and the president pulled their hoods up and followed the chef into the forest.

Anna waited a few moments, until they were surely gone, then turned to Suvi, who was furiously pushing Anna's hand away from her mouth.

"Sorry," Anna muttered, pulling her hand away and taking a steadying breath. "Guys, the Not-Deer, Kurt Mackenzie—"

"*Kurt Mackenzie!*" squealed Rosario, smiling more widely than Anna thought was possible for a human to do. "He's even better looking in person!"

"He also had an eye in the middle of his forehead," Anna reminded her. "Kind of the biggest ick of all time, Rosario."

Rosario shrugged. "Everyone has their flaws."

"What was that for?" Suvi asked, backing away and glaring at Anna.

"Covering your mouth?" asked Anna, still light-headed with fear from the Not-Deer and excitement from seeing Kurt as she pushed herself to her feet. "I didn't know how they were going to react to us spying on them. They clearly had . . . something going on that they didn't want most people to know about. They mentioned that they could turn invisible and had *literal* third eyes. They're *obviously* related to supernatural stuff. We can't just walk up to them and ask questions about the situation. Long story short, I had to cover your mouth when you shouted."

Suvi furrowed her brow. "Why didn't you let me talk to them? I had questions to ask about their ritual! I want to know how they're going to summon a ghost!"

Anna frowned and turned to Rosario, who seemed equally confused.

"You want to know how to summon a ghost?" asked Rosario.

"That's, like, insanely dangerous," Anna said. "You know that's insanely dangerous, right?"

Suvi started laughing now. "You guys are messing with me."

"We're not." Anna slid her golf club into her backpack. "Ghosts can be deadly if you aren't on guard. If you get too close, you can catch Ghost Lurgy. You get the chills, and your mind gets foggy, and all of your worst thoughts invade your brain."

"Ghosts aren't dangerous," interrupted Suvi, waving Anna off. "I mean, ghosts may look a little *weird*, but they're still people."

"They're not people," corrected Anna. "They're *ghosts*."

Suvi gazed at Anna suspiciously. "I don't know."

"You've gotta be really careful when you deal with this sort of thing." Anna thought back to the Not-Deer—the hideous way its mouth stretched back as it smiled at her. That had been her first real supernatural encounter. She'd been careless, and she'd broken the number one rule of hunting: to engage any supernatural being, incapacitate it, and kill it. What if it had gone rogue and hurt her friends? What if the Not-Deer had charged? Anna shook her head. She'd have to do better if they came across another cryptid.

"We should try to catch up with the secret society people," said Anna. "Billy ripped a page about secret societies out of Diligence's diary. I bet it included information on the Order of the Third Eye. He must've realized that there's some connection between the Order members' ability to turn invisible and the Watcher's ability to turn invisible. I bet he's heading to the Grand Ritual to figure out how they do it—to see if that'll help him see the Watcher when she's invisible, or reverse her invisibility spell, or something."

"Do you think the Watcher's still spying on us?" Suvi asked.

Anna grimaced. The watching feeling still hadn't subsided. It was like Anna was on a stage, acting out a play for someone else's entertainment.

"She's definitely watching us," Rosario answered. "Ever since we got to the forest—" Rosario looked around sheepishly. "I don't know. It feels like the trees have eyes."

Anna nodded, avoiding looking at the trees, which seemed to be standing at attention. She imagined Billy wandering the forest on his own, the Watcher examining his every move, waiting for the moment he got "boring"—waiting for the perfect moment to strike. She checked her watch. There were less than three hours left until midnight.

"We need to find Billy," said Anna, "like, as *soon* as we can."

"Okay," said Suvi. "Find Billy. Mission clearly understood. Just don't stop me the next time I try to talk to someone. I've got some questions I need answered."

Suvi then set off in the direction of the Grand

Ritual, jumping and clicking her heels together as she moved deeper into the forest.

"What's up with her?" Anna whispered to Rosario.

"I'm not sure," Rosario answered, moving to follow, "but I imagine we'll find out soon."

11

Tails and Teeth

Two Hours and Forty Minutes until Midnight

Anna was just about to ask Rosario and Suvi if they had any M&M's left when she heard Rosario gasp behind her.

Anna spun around, brandishing her golf club.

"Footprint," said Rosario, pointing at the mud in front of her.

Anna felt a swift breeze. Faster than a blink, Suvi was kneeling beside Rosario, her flashlight trained on a footprint. "What is it? Pukwudgie? Snallygaster?" She examined the footprint closely, then cocked her head to the side like a dog that had just received a command it didn't understand. "Uh, hey, Anna."

"Yeah?"

"I think Billy lost his shoes."

"Lost his *what*?" Anna zipped over to Suvi.

Sure enough, there was a bare human footprint imprinted in the thick layer of mud.

Anna frowned. Billy loved his lace-up leather boots. He would never give them up on purpose. Someone, or rather *something*, had to have taken them. Billy must have already found himself in serious trouble.

"Don't worry," said Rosario. "In order to make a footprint, Billy would have to be alive and well enough to walk. He's made it this far without dying or being seriously injured. This is a good sign."

Anna nodded and slid her golf club into her backpack. Rosario was right. There was still hope of finding Billy.

"Lemme examine the print for a minute," muttered Suvi, pulling a book out of her backpack. "Just need to double-check it's not a juvenile Sasquatch print, for the Ghouligans' sake."

Anna noticed Rosario studying Suvi. Her eyes were full of a distinct, soft concern that came from being part of a family that regularly talked about things like "feelings" and "emotions." Rosario motioned for Anna to follow her to a nearby tree. Anna quickly went, leaving Suvi to enjoy her deductions.

"I'm worried about Suvi," whispered Rosario once they were safely out of earshot. "It can't be a coincidence that she's obsessed with the idea of learning more about ghosts after what happened with her dad."

Anna shrugged. "Maybe her mind's just trying to cope with her dad dying by denying it or something? Suvi might think she'll be able to see her dad again if he's a ghost."

Rosario glanced nervously at Suvi, who was now examining Billy's footprint as if she were the Crocodile Hunter and it was a prime specimen of Australian reptile. "So, Suvi's *denying* that her dad died? Can minds even do that?"

"Well, I don't actually know. I just guessed."

"Wouldn't she tell us if she wanted to see her dad in ghost form?" Rosario wrinkled her nose. "Why would she keep that a secret?"

At the mention of keeping secrets, Anna was reminded of their encounter with the Not-Deer and the strange message it had told her. "You know how the Not-Deer mentioned you and Suvi having secrets and agendas or something?"

Rosario nodded. "I didn't entirely understand that bit."

"Neither did I," Anna admitted. "It said I can't trust you and Suvi, but I don't know why."

"Because it wants you to go off on your own. Both the Not-Deer and the Watcher know there's safety in numbers." Rosario crossed her arms. "If it's any help, I'm not keeping any secrets from you, and I don't think Suvi is either. Not important ones."

Anna nodded solemnly. She thought back to the fact Billy had kept his plan to hunt the Watcher secret from her—that he hadn't included her. She hated that he didn't trust her with important information, especially because it had landed them all in trouble. Anna hoped Suvi and Rosario weren't keeping secrets from her too.

Rosario sighed. "So, we almost met Kurt Mackenzie!"

A shiver went up Anna's spine. She was starting to understand why people said to never meet your heroes. "How about him being in a secret society? The whole third-eye thing?"

"And him helping the president with his debates? Can you imagine how smart you'd have to be to pull off a ruse like that?"

Anna crossed her arms. "You still have a crush on him, don't you?"

"How could I not?" asked Rosario. "If anything, this just goes to show he's even *more* talented than we originally thought he was."

It was then that Anna heard the growl.

She and Rosario whipped around, facing the thick group of trees and underbrush just behind them.

"Guys!" shouted Suvi excitedly. She ran up and tugged them in the direction of the footprint. "It wasn't a Sasquatch! I think I know which way Billy went!"

"Not now," muttered Anna, listening intently.

"Oh, that's nice," said Suvi sarcastically. "I find something useful that may help us find Billy, and you won't even look—"

"Something's moving in there," whispered Rosario, pointing at the cluster of trees with a shaking hand.

Rosario was right. A great sniffing noise was growing closer, like the world's biggest hunting dog picking up a trail.

Anna drew her golf club from her bag. She held it beside her right ear with both hands. Her mind flashed with images of every canine-related cryptid and ghost she'd ever encountered in her years of study. Could it be the Beast of Bray Road? The Michigan Dogman? The Demon Dog of Valle Crucis?

Anna hoped she was overreacting. Maybe it was

just a squirrel or a rabbit or some other stupid little animal they could laugh about later.

Another growl echoed through the forest like a tremble of thunder. Anna's blood grew cold in her veins.

Squirrels couldn't growl like that.

For a second, Anna heard nothing more than the trees' whisperlike rustling, Rosario's and Suvi's breathing, and the deafening beat of her own heart.

Then a voice echoed through the forest.

"Where's—my—tail?"

The voice sounded as if the speaker had spent the last several years gargling with gravel and shards of glass. Anna tightened the grip on her golf club.

A twig snapped to their left.

She, Rosario, and Suvi jumped. Suvi held up her iPad.

"Where's—my—tail?"

The voice was nearer now. Louder. Angrier.

Rosario stepped closer to Anna, pointing her flashlight in the voice's direction. "Guys—"

"I hear it too," Anna whispered.

A shadow streaked across a tree. The three girls jumped backward. Anna felt Suvi grab her arm.

"Is that a wolf?" Rosario squeaked.

"There aren't wolves in Indiana," whispered Suvi in a voice three times above her normal octave. "It isn't a wolf."

"What is it, then?" asked Rosario.

Anna stared into the forest, raising her golf club higher as she realized what the creature was—a deadly cryptid that looked like a wolf but talked like a human, with a strange concentration on its tail.

For a moment, all was still.

"What is it?" Rosario asked.

Anna whispered as quietly as the stirring leaves, "Taileybones."

"WHERE'S—MY—TAIL?"

An enormous dark shadow careened out of the forest. Anna shouted and stumbled backward. She fell over, landing hard on her back. The light from Rosario's flashlight darted about wildly to her left. Anna scrambled away from the mass, moving back on all fours without turning from it, gripping her golf club with her right hand as Rosario's flashlight settled on a monster straight from a nightmare.

A hulking creature that looked like a cross between a Doberman, Great Dane, and black bear had entered the path. It was as tall as Anna, with pointed ears that lay flat against its skull. The hair on its back stood straight up as it growled, baring a mouth full of pointed fangs. It slowly slunk toward her, glaring with intelligent, red eyes.

"Hello, human," said Taileybones.

Anna slowly scooted backward, her heart beating somewhere near her throat, her hand still tight around the golf club.

"Can you speak?" Taileybones asked.

Anna took a shaking breath. "I—uh—yes."

"Then you shouldn't have any trouble answering my question," Taileybones growled, taking a step forward.

"Anna," whispered Suvi to her left. "This way, *slowly*."

"You know, most hellhounds don't like eating humans," mused Taileybones, ever so slowly stalking toward Anna, "but I disagree. There's a certain crunch to human bones that makes them really appetizing."

Anna's lungs seemed to wither like paper bags as her brain clambered for a response.

"Suvi, I don't know if this . . . *fellow* is going to take well to being filmed," Rosario whispered.

"*I* am a paranormal investigator," said Suvi matter-of-factly as she tapped her helmet. "*This* is Taileybones. *He's* a paranormal creature."

Taileybones turned its attention to Rosario and

Suvi. Anna saw that instead of a tail, Taileybones had a nub resembling a furry hot dog. "Hello, humans—"

It paused a moment, studying Rosario with laser-like intensity. She glared just as intensely at the hell-hound, not flinching. The creature laughed, striding purposefully toward her and Suvi. "Tell me. Any chance you've seen a tail lying around?"

"Um . . ." Rosario pursed her lips and crossed her arms awkwardly, shrugging. "I—um, I'm not entirely sure."

"You aren't *sure*?" snarled Taileybones, turning completely to face her. "How could you not be sure if you've seen a tail?"

"What if—what if we say no?"

"Then you're useless, and I'll eat you."

"And if . . . we say yes?"

"Then you know the man who stole it. If you're his enemy, I'll eat you quickly. If you're his friend, I'll eat you slowly, starting with your toes and working my way up."

"Oh," said Suvi in a voice much like a squeaky toy being sat on. "In that case, we've gotta think for a minute."

"Weigh your options carefully, human. You don't have much time left," snarled the creature.

Taileybones's attention was on Suvi and Rosario. This was Anna's chance.

Clutching her golf club, Anna slowly rose up on shaking legs. She tried to look braver and more daring than she felt as she inched forward, certain that one day, her cousins were going to tell a story about how stupid Anna Grimsbane traveled into the Not-So-Witchless Woods and got eaten alive by one of the most dangerous cryptids known to hunters.

Anna raised her golf club.

"Pardon me," said Rosario.

Anna froze, her club still suspended in midair.

Rosario gulped. "Before we answer, I just want to state that I'm very sorry someone took your tail."

Taileybones cocked his head to the side, observing Rosario in silence. Anna ran through ideas for what to say during Rosario's eulogy. Why would Rosario try to negotiate with a cryptid as dangerous as *Taileybones*? Why couldn't she just let Anna handle it?

"What?" asked Taileybones.

"Um," said Rosario, wincing at the nub on the animal's backside, gesturing for Anna to lower her golf club. "I bet you didn't want your tail removed, seeing how you're looking for it. I'm sorry that man stole it from you."

Taileybones turned so he could face all three of

them, his eyes narrowed dangerously. "You are interesting humans, to sympathize with a hellhound. Who are you and what are you doing in the Watcher's forest on Halloween night?"

Anna coughed, trying to dislodge the nervous tickle that had crept up her throat and got stuck somewhere in the middle. "Um, this is Suvi Kumar and Rosario Ortiz-Rivera, and I'm Anna Grimsbane—"

"*Grimsbane?*" snarled Taileybones, the hair on his back standing up as he bared his teeth.

"Whoa, whoa!" shouted Anna, holding out the golf club. "What's wrong with being a Grimsbane?"

"You're a *hunter!*" said Taileybones, once again stalking toward Anna.

She knew it. Cryptids were dangerous. They were going to have to fight.

Anna drew her club back.

"Anna isn't a hunter!" shouted Rosario suddenly, jumping between Anna and Taileybones. She spread her hands out, one pointed at each of them like a *Jurassic Park* raptor trainer.

"I am *so* a hunter!" protested Anna. "Get out of the way!"

"A Grimsbane who isn't a hunter?" asked Taileybones.

"She likes to think she's a hunter," explained Rosario, "but she's only twelve, so her family won't let her do any hunting."

"Which is *real* unfortunate," said Suvi, kicking at a patch of dried leaves, "because I've interviewed her a few times for my YouTube channel, but no one watches the videos because she has no real authority."

Anna sputtered. "I do *so* have authority!"

Taileybones paused, standing up slightly. "You—you're *pups*?"

Rosario and Anna exchanged confused glances.

"We're kids, if that's what you're asking," said Rosario.

Something flickered behind Taileybones's eyes, a sort of softness escaping from their fiery depths as he examined Anna, Suvi, and Rosario. The hellhound took a heaving breath and plopped down, still as tall as Anna even when sitting.

"Why are you in the forest *alone*?" he asked, his rasping voice less harsh than before. "Where are your parents?"

They put you into a wooden box,
And cover you over with earth and rocks.

Anna looked to Suvi and Rosario. The forest was singing again. The same haunting melody as before.

Taileybones's eyes grew wide as he turned about the trees, searching for the source of the music. He sniffed the air, then growled.

All goes well for about a week,
Then your coffin begins to leak.

Taileybones slowly turned to the girls. "So, you've managed to make the Watcher your enemy?"

Suvi's jaw dropped. "The *trees* are the Watcher?"

"What?" Taileybones shook his head. "No. The Watcher is a friend of the forest—all of the plants and animals that reside here. The older trees are recounting their memories on her behalf, for some reason—something we're all far too young to remember." Taileybones turned to Anna. "I imagine it has something to do with your family."

Anna opened her mouth to respond but hesitated.

"Why exactly are you in the forest?" asked Taileybones.

A second ago, Taileybones had seemed pretty intent on eating her and was probably still thinking about it, even if he seemed calmer. However, he hadn't pounced on them yet. Anna saw no harm in vaguely answering his question.

"We're looking for someone," said Anna, "and we can't leave until we find him."

"Another pup?"

Anna nodded. "He's headed toward a Grand Ritual we heard some members of the Order of the Third Eye talking about. He realized there's some connection between the Order members' ability to turn invisible and the Watcher's, so he's going there to figure it out. The Watcher's got her eyes on him."

Taileybones grunted and stood. "I will help you find this other pup and escort you from the forest immediately afterward."

Anna was about to protest but held her tongue. Though hellhounds were dangerous, they were also incredible trackers. Plus, there were other dangerous cryptids in the forest, and an ally the size of a small car was nothing to sleep on. Anna knew she was supposed to hunt every cryptid she came across, but if she was careful, Taileybones could help her find Billy. Taileybones provided a strategic advantage, and they needed all the help they could get.

For now, Anna would let him help, but the second he showed any sign of endangering her, Suvi, or Rosario, Anna would be ready to fight.

"We should start walking," said Taileybones. "There are other cryptids in the forest, and most aren't as forgiving as I am."

"Well, you're the scariest of them all, right?" asked Suvi quickly, shoving her iPad in the hellhound's face now that he was no longer considering eating them. "I mean, nothing could challenge you?"

Taileybones barked in a way that resembled a laugh. "A nice thought, but unfortunately untrue. Though I am the biggest hellhound, I am certainly not the most terrifying cryptid—far from it, in fact, so you better not fall behind. After all, I am not the only one hunting humans tonight."

With that, Taileybones set off into the trees, his nublike tail wagging behind him.

12

A Terrible Tale

Two Hours and Twenty Minutes until Midnight

Correct me if I'm wrong," whispered Rosario, "but is Suvi trying to interview Taileybones?"

Rosario was, unfortunately, quite right.

"So tell me, Taileybones," said Suvi, shoving her iPad into the cryptid's face like a paparazzo, "how many people have you eaten?"

"A few," answered Taileybones gruffly.

"Fascinating. And tell me, Taileybones, do you prefer eating people to other animals?"

Taileybones was startlingly silent. For a moment, Anna thought he was going to snap and eat Suvi, until he growled, "I prefer deer."

Anna let out a breath and stepped over a large

puddle. Her foot squelched into the muddy forest floor as she trudged along the trenchlike path. She stuffed an empty Twix wrapper in her pocket, trying to drown out Suvi's interview and the trees' faint singing. They sang the same creepy song over and over and over again, humming about hearses and worms and corpses. It was getting unnerving.

Taileybones glided in front of her, eerily silent despite the muddy path. He moved gracefully through the trees as if he were dancing, a black shadow barely visible in the moonlight. Anna, Suvi, and Rosario did their best, plodding alongside him, stepping carefully to avoid twisting their ankles on the uneven ground.

What could Taileybones be thinking about? Anna shuddered at the thought. Suvi and Rosario may have trusted the cryptid, but Anna knew better. He had to be hiding something. He just had to be more dangerous than he was letting on.

It was time to see what her family had to say on the matter.

Anna quietly slipped off her backpack, pulled out Diligence's diary, opened it, and clicked on her flashlight, scanning the table of contents for anything pertaining to hellhounds.

Taileybones, hellhound, recorded by Lillian Grimsbane, age 16, 1934.

Anna glanced up at Taileybones, studying his graceful movements for any sign he was paying attention to her. Certain the hellhound was focused on the trail ahead, Anna trained her flashlight on the diary, flipped to the section on Taileybones, and began to read.

> Taileybones is a hellhound that roams the wilds of North America. We were called by Ephraim Sikes, a single man living in Holmstead, Nebraska. His letter started by describing the strange behavior of his neighbor, Jacob Townsend, shortly before Townsend's death.
>
> Townsend became increasingly erratic after a day of hunting. The night of Townsend's death, Sikes witnessed a creature we Grimsbanes know to be a hellhound crawl out of a hole it clawed in Townsend's cabin wall. The hellhound asked Sikes if he had seen its tail. Terrified, Sikes shut

his blinds, locked his door, and called
the police. In the twenty minutes it
took the police to reach his house, the
hellhound stalked around his cabin,
scratching the siding and asking
if the man had seen its tail. After
doing some research, I have concluded
that there have been at least fifteen
reports of murder by this particular
hellhound, all of which feature a
tailless hellhound of above-average
size who can communicate using
human language. Engage, incapacitate,
and kill if in a group, and do not
attempt to communicate with—

"If you wanted to know more about me, why didn't
you ask?"

Anna jumped and looked up. Taileybones glided
beside her, reading over her shoulder with an annoy-
ingly amused expression.

Anna snapped the diary shut and sped up, her
cheeks glowing red with embarrassment. Typical
cryptid behavior. Sneakily reading over her shoulder.
Trying to get the jump on her.

Taileybones let out a barking laugh, easily catching up with Anna. "Be pragmatic, Grimsbane. Surely you don't believe that garbage."

"My family's diary isn't *garbage*," said Anna defensively.

Taileybones rolled his fiery eyes. "It would, of course, be impossible for a hunter's account to be biased against a cryptid. They would *never* side with a human. That would make too much sense."

"You don't know what you're talking about."

"Don't I?" asked Taileybones. "After all, I was there, and this Lillian Grimsbane character wasn't."

"You tried to kill us earlier," Anna retorted. "That doesn't exactly make you trustworthy."

"Your people have tried to kill me and my kind for years."

"Only when they try to kill us!"

"Is that so?"

"Obviously!"

Taileybones studied her skeptically. "Your family has never sought out a benevolent spirit or cryptid? No human has ever done that?"

Anna scoffed. There was no such thing as a benevolent spirit or cryptid. "There's—"

"Have you ever considered that we cryptids might have families?"

Anna went silent, unsure how to respond.

"Have you ever considered that we, like you, might have loved ones who we want to protect?"

Anna stared at Taileybones.

"Would you like to hear my side of the story?" he asked.

Anna looked down at Diligence's diary. Curiosity worked through her brain like a worm as she ran her hand over the diary's leather cover.

What if there was something about Taileybones her family had forgotten to write? Wasn't it her job as a hunter to gather as much information as she could to put in the diary?

Anna shrugged. "I guess."

Taileybones sighed an old, heavy sigh that fell upon Anna's heart like a dumbbell. She heard many people sigh like that in the funeral home. It was a sigh of grief and mourning. Anna furrowed her brow. What could a cryptid possibly have to be sad about?

"Nearly one hundred years ago," began Taileybones, "I lived in a pack of hellhounds. A huge family. I had a wife and son. We spent every day together, hunting animals, traveling, running through the wild-flower fields and meadows near our forest. We were happy. We lived peacefully. Everything was perfect until they came.

"People—humans—began to settle in our forest. People with guns and knives and iron who were vastly unprepared for the wild. They were willing to eat anything they could get their hands on, including cryptids. We heard rumors of cryptids disappearing, of hellhounds and other packs vanishing in a flash of gunpowder, but we didn't listen. We didn't think to move. We didn't think much of anything until it was too late.

"The first hunters came at night—not hunters like you, of course. Hunters looking for food. They killed nearly half of my pack in one day. We were caught off guard, but I believe it went beyond survival for the hunters at some point. At some point it became sport, and at that point my wife died."

Anna took a sharp breath. "I—"

"My son grew angry," continued Taileybones. "He knew that Old Jake Townsend was the one who had led the raid on our pack. I told him not to upset the humans. He told me I was a coward for not avenging his mother. That night, he set off to kill Old Jake. I woke up and discovered he was missing. I tried to stop him, but by the time I got there, I was too late. Old Jake had killed him, eaten him, and buried his bones."

Anna gasped. "But—"

"When I entered the cabin and saw my son's pelt, I knew what Old Jake had done. He left me alone in this world, without my family, completely cut off from everyone I ever loved. I refused to let that happen to anyone else. In order to stop Old Jake from continuing his attacks against my pack, I killed him. Lost my tail in the process, though."

Taileybones flicked his stunted tail.

"I've been hunting humans who journey too far into the forest, the land of cryptids, ever since."

"Hunting humans?"

"Not children or families. Just hunters and those who stray too far from civilization," clarified Taileybones. "I only hunt humans who might hurt cryptids. I cannot let what happened to my family happen to someone else."

Anna sighed, the freezing mud splashing under her battered tennis shoes as the path grew steeper. She thought back to the funeral home, to her parents and siblings and aunts and uncles and cousins. She thought back to Billy. Anna had never known life without them—had never known a life without the constant company and support that came from a big family. Anna couldn't imagine someone taking that away from her.

"I'm sorry," she said in a quiet voice.

Taileybones didn't respond. Anna couldn't really blame him.

They walked beside each other in thick, foggy silence, their differences hanging in the air like an invisible wall that prevented them from communicating. Anna was a human who hunted cryptids. Taileybones was a cryptid who hunted humans. There was very little they could talk about without it being awkward.

"My brother's the one we're looking for," said Anna, in a desperate attempt to fill the silence.

"Your brother?" asked Taileybones.

Anna nodded. "I'm assuming you know about the Grimsbane curse."

Taileybones shook his head.

Anna sighed. "Well, it started when my family first came to the United States from England. Reverend Perseverance Grimsbane settled here, met my ten-times great grandma, fell in love, and got married. They were happy together for a solid five years, but one Halloween, the Watcher appeared at their house. Perseverance saw a random woman outside looking lost. He left the cabin to see if she needed help, and the Watcher decided to have some fun. Killed him and cursed all his male descendants and any man who joins the Grimsbane family to die horrible, miserable deaths. His wife—Diligence—and two daughters took up witch hunting to try to find the Watcher and break the curse. The Grimsbane women have continued their mission ever since, but obviously the family's been unsuccessful."

Anna continued, "My brother Billy and I turn thirteen tomorrow. In a few hours he's going to get cursed. He's not ready for that, though. None of us are." She turned Diligence's diary over in her hand. "Billy's been keeping a lot of secrets from the family. He's been researching the Not-So-Witchless Woods for God knows how long. He's been training with practice weapons. He stole this"—she slapped the diary—"and left to hunt the Watcher. Now I'm here to find Billy, kill the witch, and break the curse."

Taileybones shook his head in confusion. "Kill the witch?"

"I have to kill the Watcher," said Anna, shrugging. "If I don't, the curse won't break."

"That isn't how you break a curse," protested Taileybones.

"Not how you—" Anna recoiled. "What do you mean, that's not how you break a curse?"

Taileybones sighed. "Hunters are so base in their understanding of these things. Destroying the creator doesn't destroy the curse. You must undo what *caused* the curse."

"The witch caused the curse!" shouted Anna.

"Did she?"

"What's that supposed to mean?"

Taileybones shook his head. "Nothing, Grimsbane. You've proven yourself a hunter through and through, but know that if we do find the Watcher, no amount of killing is going to prevent your brother from being cursed at midnight. It's better to find him and leave the forest as soon as possible."

"But the curse is what's causing all the problems!" Anna retorted. "We *have* to hunt the Watcher!"

"Hunters caused all of *my* problems," countered Taileybones, "but I'm not eating you, am I?"

"Am I supposed to thank you for that?"

"I suppose the subtleties of humor are lost on hunters," said Taileybones. "Maybe you'll find something about jokes in that diary of yours."

They reached a clearing, and the trees stopped singing.

Taileybones froze, staring at the tree line on the other side. Anna followed his line of sight. Her breath caught in her throat.

There, just a few feet away from them, stood the Not-Deer. It smiled at Anna and Taileybones, its Cheshire grin bared all the way back to its skull. It blinked slowly with its shining, bulging eyes.

Anna removed the club from her backpack.

The Not-Deer laughed—a timbering, deep chuckle that rang through the forest.

"I see you've made a new friend, little hunter," the Not-Deer said, turning its head from side to side, examining Taileybones. "This one seems more trustworthy than the others—much more up front about his intentions."

Taileybones growled and took a step forward. His ears flattened against his head just as Rosario and Suvi entered the clearing.

"Oh, yes. Much, much more trustworthy." The Not-Deer looked Rosario and Suvi up and down. It turned back to Anna. "I have some friends of my own, and I'm very anxious for you to meet them. You see, you and your brother have made some very, very boring decisions, and the Watcher *hates* being bored. We just *have* to liven things up."

A high-pitched screech echoed through the forest. Anna instinctively looked to it.

When she looked back to the Not-Deer, it was gone.

Taileybones shot up. He stuck his nose in the air, prowling around the circle of closely knit trees, sniffing. "That's not good."

"What is it?" asked Rosario.

"Melonheads," said Taileybones.

"Melonheads?" asked Suvi, peering into the shadowed forest. "Like the ones near Lake Erie? Aren't they just weird-looking kids?"

"If kids were experimented on by an evil scientist, resulting in pointed teeth, unprecedented speed, and a desire to consume human flesh," said Anna. Melonheads were native to the region, and the Grimsbanes had hunted them for years. Anna knew just how deadly they could be.

Suvi pursed her lips. "Oh."

"Yes, *oh*."

"What do we do?" asked Suvi.

"We could run," Rosario suggested.

"We aren't running," Anna said definitively. "If we

run, they'll follow us, and they're way faster than we are. Besides, we don't want to get caught between the melonheads and another cryptid and have to fight them both at once. Better to take the melonheads on now, especially because the Watcher sent them after us. We don't want her getting any more ideas."

"There's absolutely no reason to fight them," said Rosario definitively. "We're going to negotiate first. Remember?

Anna huffed in frustration. Did Rosario not realize that these cryptids could eat them?

"You promised you'd let me try to negotiate, Anna," Rosario reminded her.

"*Fine*," Anna grumbled. "First, we'll oh so kindly ask the killer cryptids not to eat us, but when that doesn't work, we have to be in a defense formation—back-to-back and facing the forest. I'm not opening us up to attack for no reason."

Taileybones nodded. "Grimsbane, Suvi, get behind me. Rosario, up front."

"Wait. Wait. How come Rosario's going in front?" asked Anna. "I'm at least sort of a hunter."

"Because Rosario—"

Rosario coughed loudly, and Taileybones cleared his throat.

"Rosario is the negotiator," said Taileybones.

Anna rolled her eyes but didn't protest. She pulled Suvi next to her. Anna faced the tree line purposefully, gripping her golf club with two hands, ready to swing.

Suvi held up her iPad.

"Dude, not now!" said Anna.

Suvi laughed casually, as if she were at a football game and not about to fight a mob of angry cryptid children. "They're melonheads, Anna. I've got to get a video for *Ghouligans*!"

Before Anna could respond, she realized eyes were peering at them from the darkness.

13

A Figure in the Dark

Two Hours and Ten Minutes until Midnight

Something was watching them from behind a tree. Though the figure stood shadowed in darkness, its bulbous head made it clear that it wasn't exactly human. Anna watched as the creature reached out and clutched the tree with long, spidery fingers, staring at her and Suvi with catlike eyes—glowing, yellow, and unblinking.

"We've got a live one!" shouted Anna, stepping in front of Suvi.

The dark figure scuttled forward on all fours like an insect. It blinked malevolently at Anna. A wicked, white grin spread across its shadowed face.

"Metal weapon," the melonhead hissed, gesturing

to Anna's golf club with a bony hand. "Iron is not good for melonheads."

"Keep away from us and I won't have to use it!" shouted Anna, swinging the golf club in a wide arc.

"What's wrong with you?" shouted Rosario, lunging to grab the golf club.

"Huh?" Anna pulled it out of Rosario's reach while still keeping an eye on the melonhead. It took a tentative step closer, still watching Anna, as if imagining how good she'd taste with ketchup and mustard.

"He's a little kid!" protested Rosario. "You can't hit a little kid!"

Much to Anna's dismay, Rosario left the defense formation. She approached the melonhead and crouched down, reaching her hand out as if she wanted to shake the melonhead's hand. "Hi. I'm Rosario Ortiz-Rivera. What's your name?"

The melonhead hissed and stood up, still shrouded in darkness. "Humans should stay out of the forest."

Rosario withdrew her hand slowly. "Unfortunately, we can't leave just yet, buddy, but I'm glad we've found a goal we can both work toward: getting the humans out of the forest. Maybe you can help us find someone we're looking for."

"Someone to *eat*," snarled the melonhead.

Anna quickly grabbed Rosario's coat and pulled her back to the group. "Still up for negotiating, or are you going to let me fight?"

Rosario shook her head, her brow furrowed in disbelief. "We can't give up just yet. I'm making good progress."

"We have two more over here!" shouted Suvi, barely audible over the sound of Taileybones's sudden bark.

The melonhead that had talked to Rosario entered the clearing and grinned.

It didn't look much better in the moonlight.

The cryptid's eyes were shining and golden, as if someone had stuck two penlights in its large, hairless head. Its pale, translucent skin was pulled so tightly over its bulging skull that its brain was nearly visible, so much so that Anna could see blue blood rushing through its pulsing veins. The melonhead clicked its teeth—sharp, decaying, and yellowed—and took another step forward, pulling at its tattered hospital gown with filthy, bony fingers that ended in sharp points.

"Humans don't belong in the forest," the melon-head snarled as it approached. "Humans hurt us."

"Humans always hurt melonheads," moaned a voice next to Anna. She jumped and saw two more melonheads enter the clearing. They slipped forward silently, their long-nailed, dirty feet sliding through the layers of decaying leaves and mud on the forest floor.

Anna swung the golf club in another arc, driving the hissing melonheads farther back.

"Anna, stop!" Rosario protested.

Anna ignored her. Regardless of her promise to Rosario, Anna had to keep the melonheads away from the group—away from her friends.

"Humans put poison in our brains," snarled a melonhead, once again starting forward.

"Poison in our hearts!" screamed another. "Poor, sick orphans made into science experiments!"

"We ran into the wilds. Into the woods, where no one could hurt us again," whispered the melonhead directly in front of Anna, its sick grin growing ever wider.

"But now you humans are here," said another, "with your iron weapons."

"We won't be hurt again," they echoed in unison, hissing and snarling as they closed in.

Anna gritted her teeth and gripped her golf club, ready to hit a melonhead out of the park. She wasn't going to let them hurt Suvi and Rosario.

A melonhead lurched forward.

Anna closed her eyes and swung.

An earsplitting crack broke through the clearing, accompanied by a smell like burning tires and a howl of pain.

"Anna!" Rosario shouted—her uncharacteristically loud burst of anger startling Anna to attention.

Anna opened her eyes and saw the melonhead scampering away on its back, clutching its dislocated shoulder tightly as smoke coiled from the place Anna had hit—a distinct line of red etched into its pale skin. Tears ran from the melonhead's yellow eyes, tracing wobbling lines in the grime that covered its pale face.

Anna tried to ignore the way her stomach sank to her shoes when she saw what she'd done.

"Three more over here!" yelled Suvi.

"C'mon!" Anna shouted at the melonheads, swinging her golf club wildly at them. "Is that the best you've got?"

"Don't provoke them, Grimsbane!" yelled Taileybones.

Anna ignored him, cracking another melonhead on its gnarled foot. It howled and retreated. Anna scrunched up her nose at the smell of burning flesh.

"Anna, stop!" yelled Rosario, grabbing at Anna's golf club.

Anna moved it out of her reach, standing on her toes. "They're attacking us! You expect me to just sit here and let them kill us?"

"*You're* the one attacking *them*!"

"Hurting poor melonheads," hissed the melonhead farthest from Anna, narrowing its eyes. "Kill the hunter first."

"We can still talk this out!" Rosario implored, holding her hands out to the melonheads. "We can fix this!"

The branches leaned and shook in a violent wind that seemed to have appeared out of nowhere, picking the leaves off the ground and scattering them about the clearing. Nearly a dozen melonheads emerged from the forest, their claws raised, poised to strike. As Anna had predicted, negotiations had failed. There was no negotiating with cryptids as deadly and dangerous as melonheads. Anna grasped her golf club. They were completely surrounded. There was only one option: engage, incapacitate, kill.

It was then that something short, heavy, and rock-like shot from the treetops. It landed in front of Anna with a thud.

Suvi's flashlight flicked to it. Anna's jaw dropped in horror. The melonheads froze.

One of the most dangerous cryptids in North America stood in front of her—a waist-high imp in a plaid, three-piece suit that clashed horribly with his fire-engine red skin, horns, and talons. He glared at the melonheads with completely black eyes, running a clawed hand through his neatly styled black hair.

"*Boo*," he whispered.

"RUN!" screamed a melonhead. "RUN!"

The shrieking melonheads staggered to their knees. They retreated into the forest, crying and howling, dragging their injured comrades behind them as the Nain Rouge stepped forward.

Anna held her golf club up until the melonheads were out of sight. She looked down at the imp, unsure whether it was safer to bow or run.

The Detroit branch of the Knights of Van Tassel had been hunting the Nain Rouge for centuries, though they were obviously far less than successful. Events like tremendous ice storms, the Detroit riots, and the fall of the city's founder himself were all due to the cryptid, known for his pleasure at the misery of those who insulted him.

"Taileybones, I thought I heard your growling among the cries of the melonheads," said the Nain Rouge in a thick French accent. He smiled up at Anna,

Suvi, and Rosario with three rows of pointed, shark-like teeth. "Who are these young mademoiselles?"

"You, sir, are looking at Suvi Kumar, Rosario Ortiz-Rivera, and Anna Grimsbane," said Taileybones as he plopped down into a sitting position.

"Grimsbane?" The Nain Rouge's expression darkened as he narrowed his eyes at Anna, examining her the same way a scientist would examine a specimen under a microscope. "Like the hunters?"

He snapped his fingers.

A powerful, ancient energy began emanating from the cryptid, reaching greedily toward Anna's heart with cold, grasping fingers. She felt the hair on her arms stand up, a slight electricity invisibly etching its way through the air. Her breath came out in puffs of white smoke.

"She's too young to hunt," said Taileybones.

The Nain Rouge grinned. His shark teeth glinted in the light of Suvi's flashlight. For a moment, Anna thought he was going to attack, but then he clapped his hands jovially.

"Well, thank heavens for that," said the imp, giving a hearty chuckle. "We still might have time to save your spirit."

The energy retreated and Anna gasped, the chill

leaving her body with a sudden whoosh.

The Nain Rouge sighed, placing his hands on his hips as he looked up at Anna, Suvi, Rosario, and Taileybones. "How did the four of you manage to draw the ire of the melonheads?"

"It's kind of a long story," said Anna, staring down at the imp. "We were just walking past and—"

Her breath caught in her throat.

There, upon the Nain Rouge's too-small feet, was a pair of well-worn, lace-up leather boots. Anna had only ever known one person with a pair of shoes like that.

"Um—" Anna coughed, clearing her throat. "Mr. Nain Rouge, sir, if you don't mind me asking, where did you get those shoes?"

The Nain Rouge shrugged. "A boy dressed as an Irish sheep farmer."

Billy.

"He gave you his shoes?" asked Anna in disbelief.

"And his flashlight," added the Nain Rouge, producing a small red flashlight from his back pocket.

Anna's lungs deflated like a balloon. "Why would he give you his flashlight?"

The Nain Rouge shrugged, pocketing Billy's flashlight. "Because I asked. Everyone with a brain knows better than to say *non* to the Nain Rouge."

"Is he all right?" Anna asked desperately, her mind flooded with images of barefoot Billy encountering all the cryptids they had by himself. "I mean, he wasn't hurt or anything? Did he look okay?"

"Can you please describe what happened when you encountered the boy?" added Rosario, who had been respectfully silent the entire time the Nain Rouge was talking. "What he did? Where he was going?"

Anna gulped, looking to Rosario. Anna had done as she'd promised. She'd let Rosario try to negotiate before attacking. The melonheads were dangerous, and they had attacked her friends. Anna had needed to defend Suvi and Rosario, right? She was certain she'd done the right thing, even if her mind swung back to the image of the injured melonhead crawling away from her with tears in its eyes.

The Nain Rouge nodded. "Of course. I was lounging in a tree earlier this evening when I saw the boy pass by. He was using a flashlight. I see the flashlight. I see the shoes. I want them. I ask. He gives. He goes on his way."

"Did you see which way he went?" asked Rosario.

The Nain Rouge nodded. "Oui, I did. He was heading toward the 'Grand Ritual'"—the Nain Rouge made mocking air quotes with his claws—"near the center of the forest—a brave direction for such a fragile-looking boy."

Anna felt a strange mixture of relief and fear. Relief, because at least they'd confirmed Billy was going to the Grand Ritual. Fear, because he was heading into a ritual where people were planning on summoning a ghost. Didn't Billy know how deadly Ghost Lurgy could be?

Suvi cleared her throat and raised her iPad slightly. "Speaking of the Grand Ritual, Mr. Nain Rouge, sir, do you know anything about ghosts?"

The Nain Rouge furrowed his eyebrows so deeply they nearly touched. "Do I know anything about what?"

"Ghosts," said Suvi, adjusting the zoom so the Nain Rouge's face was in focus. "I have what you might call a professional interest in all things supernatural, but I'm specifically curious about ghosts. Life after death, talking to spirits—that sort of thing."

Anna raised her eyebrows and turned to Rosario. They were clearly thinking the same thing—the tiff between them forgotten in the face of the current issue. There was no way Suvi was asking this question for general ghost-hunting reasons. This was definitely about her dad.

"Yikes," Anna muttered.

Rosario nodded in agreement.

The Nain Rouge shook his head dismally. "I'm afraid you don't want to know too much about that."

Suvi's smile wavered. "What do you mean, I don't want to know about it?"

"The mysteries of life and death are largely unknown and extremely complicated," explained Taileybones, scratching his ear with his back paw. "It is easy to get bogged down in the particulars, to get lost in the mysteries—especially for humans, who are guaranteed death after a very short time. People who spend their lives trying to understand or avoid the mysteries of death often forget to live."

"My family runs a funeral home and hunts ghosts for a living, and we seem just fine," retorted Anna. She instantly regretted bringing up hunting upon seeing the pained expression on Taileybones's face. "I mean—we do, though."

"You're a member of the family that kills cryptids and hunts witches to keep their men alive," stated the Nain Rouge, gesturing to Anna with a flourish. "Is that not an obsession with death?"

"We hunt to make sure the men in my family and other humans stay safe and protected, if that's what you're asking," corrected Anna, suppressing the urge to skewer the Nain Rouge with her golf club. "I'm sure you'd do the same if someone hurt your family."

Taileybones nodded. "I certainly did."

Anna and Taileybones made eye contact and instantly glanced away. Anna felt her cheeks growing warmer and looked down, embarrassed about having something in common with him. Taileybones was a cryptid, after all.

The Nain Rouge turned back to Suvi and continued, "I won't answer questions about death, and I suggest you move on to a more tangible topic of interest."

Anna glanced at Suvi, who was resolutely staring at her shoes, biting her bottom lip. "Sir, I am well aware of the difficult nature of death."

Anna breathed heavily through her nose, desperate to change the conversation before it got too emotional. "Well, that's great, but we're actually out here looking for someone. Did the boy mention *why* he was going to the Grand Ritual?"

The Nain Rouge shrugged. "Oui, he was headed to the ritual to find Hot Foot Powder."

Taileybones snarled.

"What?" asked Anna, turning from the imp to the hellhound, surprised at his reaction. "What's Hot Foot Powder?"

"Hot Foot Powder is a material that some witches create that allows them to turn themselves or any object invisible," answered the Nain Rouge. "Only people who use Hot Foot Powder themselves can see past it. The Order of the Third Eye has studied it, and many members carry it with them, in case of emergencies."

Taileybones narrowed his eyes slightly at Anna, as if looking for some minute reaction from her. Anna was confused by his behavior at first, but felt her confusion turn to anger as clues began to click in her mind like pieces in a puzzle. Billy was heading to the Grand Ritual to get Hot Foot Powder, a material that could make witches turn invisible. Billy must've realized the Watcher was using Hot Foot Powder to vanish whenever the Grimsbanes got close. *That's* why Billy was heading to the Grand Ritual—so that he could use Hot Foot Powder to see the Watcher—so she couldn't vanish from his view. The Watcher wouldn't be able to escape if the people hunting her *also* used Hot Foot Powder.

And based on Taileybones's reaction to the Nain Rouge's revelation, Taileybones had known about this the whole time but had refrained from telling Anna.

Anna huffed, crossing to the hellhound. "You knew why Billy was going to the Grand Ritual! You *knew* he was looking for Hot Foot Powder, and you didn't think to mention it?"

"The goal is to find your brother and escort you out of the forest," said Taileybones matter-of-factly. "Not to find the Watcher."

"Have you thought that maybe I might *want* to kill the Watcher after all she's done to my family?"

Taileybones snarled, "There are many cryptids in this forest who could say the same thing about Grimsbanes."

"Anna isn't killing any witches," said Rosario definitively, crossing her arms and nodding at Anna. "She *promised* we'd try to negotiate, though that promise seemed to have slipped her mind when it came to the melonheads."

Anna rolled her eyes. "Why are you so against me killing witches?"

"Because I—" Rosario paused, took a deep breath, and straightened her coat. "Because I don't think that anyone should be killed for no good reason. Especially not by three seventh graders and a hellhound."

"No good reason?" asked Anna. "You don't think

breaking the curse is a good reason to kill the Watcher?"

"Will you all be *quiet* about the Watcher?" asked Suvi.

Everyone in the clearing turned to her. In the silence, Anna could hear the trees resume their song.

> *And the worms crawl out and the*
> *worms crawl in.*
> *The worms that crawl in are lean*
> *and thin.*
> *The ones that crawl out are fat*
> *and stout.*
> *Your eyes fall in and your hair*
> *falls out.*

Suvi took a deep breath, closing her eyes for a moment. "It doesn't matter if we find the Watcher or not. Billy's heading toward the ritual, so we should find him and get out. This *noble gentleman*," she said, gesturing to the Nain Rouge, who looked rather pleased with the compliment, "pointed Billy in the direction of the Grand Ritual—the direction we were already heading in. Since this is a time-sensitive rescue mission, there's no time to lose."

With that, Suvi pushed past the Nain Rouge, her suspended cameras swishing behind her as she strode purposefully in the direction of the Grand Ritual, leaving her best friends and two cryptids staring at her back.

14

A Raucous Ritual

One Hour and Forty-Five Minutes until Midnight

Anna noisily flipped a page of Diligence's diary, her face screwed up in concentration as she tried to decipher a long-dead relative's sloppy handwriting in the light of her flashlight, desperate to find any hint of information on ghosts, the Grand Ritual, and Hot Foot Powder. Anna was finding it difficult to concentrate. Suvi was practically sprinting forward at the front of the group, her camera apparatus jangling noisily like out-of-tune wind chimes every time she stepped. Rosario and Taileybones were just behind, their hushed voices mingling with the soft rustle of dead leaves and the sound of a few jackalopes hopping around in the underbrush.

To make matters worse, the trees' singing had grown

louder, almost like a church choir composed exclusively of baritones was following them. It made it impossible to concentrate.

> *They'll wrap you up in a clean*
> *white sheet*
> *And put you down about six*
> *feet deep.*
> *They'll put you in a big, black box,*
> *And cover you over with earth*
> *and rocks.*

Anna sighed. She knew Rosario and Taileybones were talking about her, but she didn't care. The Watcher hurt her family—had been hurting her family for hundreds of years. Countless relatives had died because of the stupid curse. Grimsbanes had been hunting the Watcher for centuries, and none of them had ever felt bad about it, so why should Anna?

Then again, there was the problem of her actual ability to hunt. Things with the melonheads hadn't exactly gone great. Anna didn't even want to think about what could have happened if the Nain Rouge hadn't shown up. Maybe her family was right. Maybe Anna wasn't as experienced as she thought.

She turned her attention back to the diary and continued to read the margins of the section on ghosts.

Moanes and shreeks loud enough to burst the eardrums are nown to eko throughout the ghosts' chosen romping grounde. —Constance Grimsbane, 1721

Ghosts may be expelled using lavender water or iron. —Agnes Grimsbane, 1840

Remember to avoid hunting ghosts in clusters of more than three, or you'll get Ghost Lurgy. Less than ten, you'll get mild symptoms. More than ten, you could be in serious trouble. If you see a ghost, take immediate action and engage, incapacitate, kill! —Lenore Grimsbane, 1964

Taileybones howled and Anna jumped, nearly dropping the diary.

"What?" asked Suvi. Her cameras bounced noisily as she backpedaled to walk beside the hellhound. "Do you see something?"

Taileybones barked. The nub of his tail swung behind him in a definitive rhythm as he bounced to an inaudible beat. "You'll hear soon."

After walking for about ten more minutes, Anna heard the unmistakable sound of a thudding bass line echoing through the forest.

"Is that *music*?" asked Suvi in disbelief, turning around to face the group.

Anna nodded. She supposed even secret societies could appreciate a good bop every once in a while.

Rosario took a shaking breath and drew her coat closer around herself. She examined the trees with restless eyes, as if afraid one of the long branches might bend down and snatch her up.

"You all right?" Anna asked, closing Diligence's diary and sliding it back into her backpack.

"Huh?" asked Rosario, looking up. "Oh, yeah." She shrugged and smiled half-heartedly. "Just thinking."

Anna hesitated. Rosario's olive skin had gone remarkably pale. She was taking deep breaths, a sure sign something was upsetting her.

"Are you still mad at me about the whole melon-head thing?" Anna asked.

"No," Rosario said definitively. "I mean, you did let me negotiate, in all technicality." She shrugged.

"Maybe just let me negotiate for a bit longer next time."

Anna considered this. If Rosario wasn't mad about the melonhead incident, maybe she was scared. Maybe that was the secret the Not-Deer mentioned. Maybe Rosario was really scared of ghosts and was doing all this despite her fears because she was such a good friend.

"Are you worried about the ritual?" asked Anna. "Because of the ghost?"

Rosario didn't answer, which was more than enough of an answer for Anna.

"You don't have to be embarrassed about being nervous. Besides, you don't have to worry." Anna gave Rosario what she hoped was a reassuring pat on the back. "I've got the golf club, and it's custom-made—infused with iron. Any ghost comes near you, I'll dematerialize them."

Anna heard Taileybones chuckle.

"What?"

"Nothing to concern yourself with, Grimsbane."

"You don't think I'm strong enough to kill a ghost?" asked Anna, getting flashbacks to the doubt that her entire family, including Billy, had shown her through-out her life, especially prevalent in the last week.

"Of course, you, an untrained child with no real

understanding of witchcraft or the supernatural, have the ability to kill a ghost. Though this is, of course, complicated by the fact the ghost is already dead."

"I can!"

"And I agreed with you."

"Sarcastically!"

Taileybones shrugged. "If you want to think so, who am I to correct you?"

Anna exclaimed in frustration, "I was trying to be nice! Rosario's already nervous enough without you saying I'm not strong enough to hunt!"

Taileybones shook his head.

"What'd you do that for?" asked Anna. Arguing with Taileybones was remarkably like arguing with her siblings. "I'm serious."

Taileybones nodded forward, where Suvi and Rosario had stopped walking.

The largest tree Anna had ever seen in her life stood proudly ahead of them, stretching its finger-like branches at least a mile into the ink black sky. Shriveled brown leaves littered the ground, with roots as wide as Anna's arm weaving through them like snakes. A stooped opening at the center of the great trunk blazed with a cold, blue light and emanated music so loud it could wake the dead.

A wooden sign sat above the opening. Anna stepped forward to get a closer look.

FOUR HUNDRED AND THIRD ANNUAL GRAND RITUAL

"Suvi, turn off your cameras," said Rosario, who now had her pink, fur-lined hood pulled so low over her face she looked like a Barbie Sith lord.

Suvi whipped toward Rosario as if she'd suggested Suvi offer herself up as a sacrifice to the ghosts. "What about *Ghouligans*?"

Rosario shook her head. "If I know anything about secret societies, it's that they probably don't take kindly to being recorded."

"Fair enough," muttered Suvi with a grimace. She started turning off her cameras, struggling to reach the one hung over her head.

"Diligence's diary didn't say anything about cameras," Anna muttered to Suvi. "I'm sure it'd be fine if you want to film them—just try to keep it sneaky."

Taileybones chuckled. "You are aware your family isn't the be-all, end-all of information on the supernatural, aren't you?"

Anna was about to retort that her family was, in fact, the be-all, end-all of information on the supernatural and that Taileybones should mind his own business when a great roar of laughter echoed from inside the tree. All four of them turned toward the opening, as if drawn to the chilling, haunting sound that emerged from the trunk like a fog. Anna felt something inside that tree, something old and powerful that threatened to draw her in.

She thought back to her family's trip to Lake Erie, to walking along the moonless beach late at night with Mom, to the black waves lapping at her feet as if attempting to pull her into the water. Whatever was in the tree felt very much like that.

"Let's find Billy and get out," said Rosario quickly, pulling her hood farther down over her face.

Anna raised her eyebrows. She had never seen Rosario so nervous about anything in her entire life.

"You sure you're all right?" Anna asked, eyeing Rosario cautiously.

Rosario nodded. "Never better."

With that, Rosario crouched down and entered the hole in the tree, vanishing into the bright light and noise.

Anna took a deep breath and walked forward. She crouched down and gripped the trunk on either side of the entrance, staring into the smoky blue haze that divided the barrier. She'd have to be on guard. The Order was planning on summoning a ghost. Ghosts were dangerous, but if Billy was in there, Anna was willing to risk it—

"Whenever you're ready, Grimsbane," growled Taileybones.

Anna shot him a look. He shot it back to the best of his doggish ability.

Taking a deep breath, Anna ducked her head and entered the tree.

Anna had prepared for many different possibilities when she pictured the Grand Ritual. Most of these possibilities involved blood dripping from the walls as ghosts rose up from the floor, objects flying around the room, and the earth grumbling and shaking as spirits engaged in dark, dangerous activities that could seriously harm any well-meaning human. Anna thought she'd have to save the day—rescue a whole group of people from horrible, evil ghosts.

None of the visions involved the president Milly rocking.

The second Anna entered the tree, a cacophony of noise and light overwhelmed her senses. Streamers and colored lights hung from the rootlike rafters. A giant disco ball spun over a blue bonfire in the middle of the gymnasium-sized dance floor, crowded with a sea of purple-cloaked people. Anna spotted a familiar newscaster leading a conga line consisting of the entire Cleveland Cavaliers basketball team. Beside them, an Olympic gymnast told a story to a laughing country singer. Kurt Mackenzie set off a confetti cannon, whooping and hollering as the colorful bits of paper floated onto the crowd, much to the partygoers' obvious annoyance. Each person had a glowing, purple eye in the middle of their forehead.

Just above the bonfire was a digital clock ticking down from 1:30, the numbers shining like a multicolored disco dance floor. Above the clock were the words "MINUTES UNTIL GHOSTS ARRIVE!"

The ritual had already started.

Anna drew in a breath and her lungs spasmed, protesting at the intensely cold air. She drew her coat closer, wincing at the bitter cold. An overwhelming sense of dread crept upon her, anxiety clawing at her chest and throat. The music grew quiet and muted, as if she were hearing it underwater. The cold air was reaching into her soul, blurring her vision and quickening her pulse.

"Ghost Lurgy," explained Taileybones, who had entered the party just behind her, closely followed by Suvi. "Your emotions may feel stronger as well. Ghosts tend to have that effect on humans."

"How can we have Ghost Lurgy?" Anna asked. "There aren't any ghosts around."

"Not technically," said Taileybones, nodding to the fire, "but they'll be here soon. Loads of them. Some are already starting to peek through the veil."

As Anna looked at the bonfire, she noticed silvery, phantom hands stretching out from the fire before being rapidly pulled back in. It was like looking at the big screen at a concert, at all of the people in the pit reaching upward.

"This is bad," Anna noted, staring at the phantasmal fingers. "Really bad."

Taileybones nodded. "Hopefully the Ghost Lurgy won't kill you."

"*Hopefully?*" asked Suvi, already shivering. She struggled to pull her hood up, not realizing it was impossible to do with the various cameras sticking out of her helmet like antlers.

"How're we supposed to find Billy in here?" asked Anna, doing her best to take steadying breaths. She stood on her toes to try to see over a line of people bobbing for apples.

"Split up?" suggested Rosario.

"With the ritual about to end?" asked Anna, gesturing wildly toward the fire. "It's too dangerous!"

"What if we go in twos?" asked Rosario, her eyes invisible under her hood. "We'll find Billy faster if we separate. In the meantime, we should also keep an eye out for Hot Foot Powder, just in case he managed to get some and leave. I'll go with Suvi, and Taileybones can go with you."

"No," said Anna and Taileybones simultaneously.

Rosario huffed. "Oh, c'mon! I can watch Suvi, and you can watch each other!"

"Neither you nor Suvi know how to fight," said Anna. "Why would you guys go together?" Her mind turned back to the Not-Deer and its warning that Suvi and Rosario weren't trustworthy. Could Rosario's idea to separate have something to do with them keeping secrets from Anna?

"Oh please!" said Rosario, swatting Anna off. "I'm perfectly capable of handling myself. Besides, you and Taileybones will be too busy bickering to cause a scene."

With that, Rosario grabbed Suvi's hand and melted into the dancing crowd.

Without Suvi and Rosario, Anna felt that the cryptid standing beside her was more like an elephant than a hellhound. Anna examined her tennis shoes, then the crowd of cultists, then Kurt Mackenzie. Her eyes drifted everywhere but the giant beast next to her.

"It's no secret we don't enjoy each other's company," said Taileybones gruffly, breaking the silence. "It'll be in our best interests to work together to find your brother and get you home as quickly as possible, so we never have to interact again. Agreed?"

Anna breathed a sigh of relief and nodded. "Sounds like a plan."

"In all seriousness, this is an extremely unsafe situation," said Taileybones. "If the ritual ends, and the ghosts start to get a hint of your warmth, they'll absolutely lose control of themselves, by no fault of their own."

"My *warmth*?" asked Anna, snorting. "I wouldn't exactly call myself a warm-and-fuzzy person."

Taileybones rolled his eyes. "That's not what I meant. Ghosts aren't supposed to be on this side of the veil. They can only be summoned by a living human. Ghosts are perfectly comfortable on their side, but when they cross here, they *also* experience the symptoms of Ghost Lurgy, but a million times worse. They become absolutely freezing, and they lose all sense of their personhood. They'll do anything to get warm. That's why they go after humans. It's all about body heat—about feeling alive."

Anna considered this. In all the years she'd studied ghosts, she'd never come across this information. Despite this, somehow, it made sense. How had the Grimsbanes never figured this out?

Anna drew her coat even closer to herself and followed Taileybones through the crowd.

"Why don't the other people have any symptoms?" Anna asked, looking at the people partying around her.

"They're the ones who summoned the ghosts," answered Taileybones, "so they won't be affected."

"What if one of the ghosts gets out? What if they hurt someone?"

"Humans rarely care about other humans. They don't fully consider the consequences of their actions." Taileybones sighed. "They find ghosts fascinating, so they summon them."

As Anna got closer to the fire, the symptoms of Ghost Lurgy got worse. It felt like someone had placed a weight on her chest, slowly crushing her as she continued deeper.

"This sucks," Anna muttered.

Taileybones turned to look at her. If Anna hadn't known better, she could've sworn she saw something like sympathy echo in his fiery eyes. "Just focus on your brother," Taileybones said, continuing forward with his usual graceful glide. "What does he look like? I might be able to see him."

Anna nodded. Billy. She had to focus on Billy.

"He's a quarter of an inch shorter than me," said Anna. "Skinny. Dark red hair. Pale skin. Freckles on his nose." Her words hung in the cold air, floating up toward the ceiling, leaving her to join Billy, wherever he was. "He's wearing a white sweater, and he really likes reading."

"I don't see him yet," said Taileybones.

"He's really smart," continued Anna. "Like, unnaturally smart, and he's really cool, and he wants to go on adventures one day." She shuddered in the cold. "That's why he left."

Anna heard Taileybones asking some of the society members if they'd seen a boy pass through earlier, and their muttered denials. Anna's mind drifted, as if the freezing air around her were dissecting it. What if Billy never came back? What if he died in this forest? What if he was the next dead Grimsbane whose story got told to future generations of boys to keep them from taking risks?

"We got in a fight before he ran away," Anna admitted, an unmistakable waver in her voice. "We said really awful things to each other. I thought he was leaving me behind to go to some stupid party. When I found out where he'd really gone—that he was trying to hunt the Watcher—I thought I could handle it on my own, but I don't know if I can. If I'd called my mom instead of trying to find Billy myself, all the experienced hunters could've come home, even if it took them a while."

Anna's thoughts were spilling out of her mouth without her control. She was freezing. Her heart felt like it was going to shatter from the cold.

"They could've gone to find him instead," Anna muttered, "but I thought it would be better to save him on my own. I thought I'd be good at hunting, but I'm not. Everyone said I wasn't experienced enough, and I didn't believe them. They were just trying to keep me safe, just like how I was trying to keep Billy safe."

Anna felt an unpleasant prickling sensation in the back of her eyes. Her vision grew blurry, guilt scratching at the front of her throat. "If he dies, it's gonna be my fault."

It was then that Anna looked upward. Her breath hitched.

The timer had reached zero.

The ritual was already complete.

15

The Ghostly Gathering

One Hour and Twenty Minutes until Midnight

Taileybones turned to her with wide eyes and an open jaw, suddenly looking uncomfortable. "Oh. Um." He looked around the room as if trying to find a solution to Anna's tears. "Are you *crying*?"

"The timer," Anna murmured, nodding up toward it. Her head felt like it weighed a million pounds.

"That . . . makes sense." He turned back to Anna. "You have *extremely* bad Ghost Lurgy. Stay near me. We'll get out of here as soon as possible."

Anna was barely listening. All she could think about was Billy—about the hours they'd spent with their friends at the Blue Moon, the trouble they'd caused at school, arguing with him just before he left.

All he'd wanted to do was to go on an adventure. All he'd wanted to do was prove he was capable to those who doubted him, the same way Anna did. Why had Anna argued with him? Why had she assumed she was more skilled than she actually was?

"It's gonna be my fault," Anna repeated, feeling a sob echo through her chest. "He's gonna die if I can't do this. I didn't talk to him after the fight. We're never going to make up. My family said I was too young to hunt, and they were right."

"Oh my." Taileybones grimaced uncomfortably. "I do not handle emotions well—um." He winced, nudging her forward with his paw. "Everything will be fine. We'll find Billy soon. Just keep moving."

Anna nodded, leaning in to him a bit, drawn to the warmth of his fur. Though she felt Taileybones flinch, he didn't complain. He just continued walking, Anna right beside him.

Taileybones was nice.

He was a cryptid.

Why was he being nice and not eating her?

Anna sighed shakily. "I'm really confused."

Taileybones nodded. "If it makes you feel any better, I am too."

It was then that Anna felt a sharp chill on her

shoulder. Before she could respond, a strong hand pulled her backward into a horrific scene.

A shining woman stood over Anna, gripping her shoulder with sharp, talonlike fingernails. The woman's floor-length, white wedding gown hung limply on her emaciated frame. A ruined veil covered her long, black hair, curtaining her gaunt, pale face like a burial shroud.

None of this would have scared Anna if it weren't for the woman's eyes.

The ghost bride's eye sockets were completely empty—hollows with no clear back—just pure darkness, reaching endlessly into a void. Despite this, silvery tears traced down her cheeks, dripping off her sharp jawline and over her cruel smile, bared directly at Anna.

"Didn't realize someone was bringing life to the party," the bride said, her voice resonating as if she had spoken in an empty church and not on a raging dance floor. "You're so warm." She dug her chilling fingers into Anna's shoulder. "*So* warm."

Anna wheezed in response, her sense of dread growing stronger, her mind becoming as cold and chaotic as the air around her.

As Anna looked behind the bride, she saw a sea of

silvery ghosts mixed among the secret society members, all in varying states of decay. Some looked barely more than skeletons. Some couldn't have been dead more than a few hours. Some were missing limbs. They didn't seem to notice the society members, who were gazing around in wonder, but they did notice Anna. The ghosts turned to one another, muttering and pointing at her.

Anna tried to muster up the energy to reach for her golf club, but she simply couldn't. It felt like her soul was being leached out of her body by the bride's steel-tight grip, growing stronger and more pronounced by the second.

The bride closed her eyelids. The thin skin sank into her eye sockets as she ran a freezing, bony hand through Anna's hair. She inhaled deeply, a hollow imitation of life. "How lovely it must be to feel alive."

Another ghost reached out and grabbed Anna's wrist.

She gasped at the sudden cold, her gaze falling on a sailor with bloated skin, bulging eyes, and pale blue lips. His grip tightened.

"So alive," he whispered, water dribbling from his mouth and onto Anna's exposed wrist. "So warm."

She felt another ghost grab her other shoulder.

Taileybones's paw wrapped around her middle and pulled her back. "We need to get out of here."

Anna wanted to act, but she felt so weak, she could hardly keep her eyes open. They were surrounded, but why did it matter? They were here for an important reason, but everything was growing colder. . . .

"Don't go," implored the bride, stalking toward Anna and Taileybones. The corpselike ghosts followed closely behind her. "Please don't go."

"I'm afraid we aren't planning on staying long," said Taileybones, backing up and dragging Anna with him. "We're here searching for another human. A boy."

"A boy? It's just her and the other girls here," said a young woman's ghost. Silver blood dripped from an axe embedded in her chest, dribbling onto her white dress. She reached her hands toward Anna. "They're so warm. I want to be *warm*."

"Billy," muttered Anna. Her brother's face swam across her vision. He hadn't made it to the ritual. How could he not have made it to the ritual if he was ahead of them? Did that mean he was—

"Found Hot Foot Powder," sang Rosario, emerging from the crowd with Suvi, who looked as pale and miserable as Anna felt. Rosario held up a ziplock bag full of what looked like peppercorns and dirt, smiling under her hood.

The ghosts backed up as if Rosario were a chaperone at a middle school dance. A slight but audible growl escaped Taileybones's throat as he stared at the ziplock, his eyes narrowing maliciously.

"Oh, Anna, you look awful," murmured Rosario.

"We need to go," said Taileybones quickly, nudging Anna into Rosario. Anna stumbled, but Rosario caught her, holding her up with both hands. Anna's head bobbed sideways as her vision began to go in and out of focus. Her breath was shallow.

Anna felt one of her arms being looped around Rosario's shoulder.

"Where's Billy?" asked Rosario. Her voice sounded distant, like she was shouting through a tunnel.

"Not here," answered Taileybones. "Let's get them out."

They slowly moved through the party. The ghosts gave them a wide berth as Rosario made her way through the crowd.

"Yeah, don't like Hot Foot Powder, do you?" Rosario shouted, shaking the bag like a maraca.

"What're you doing?" Suvi whispered, hanging on to Rosario's other side.

"My best," answered Rosario. "Let's get you guys out of here before you freeze to death."

16

Questions of Death

One Hour and Five Minutes until Midnight

Anna stepped outside the tree and immediately fell onto all fours, gasping in the chilly fall air like a fish thrown back into a lake. Sensation returned to her fingertips. The cloudiness in her brain began to dissipate. Her eyes still struggled to focus on the damp, leaf-strewn ground. Freezing mud wove between her fingers as she gripped the earth, trying to catch her breath.

Rosario patted her on the back. "You're doing just fine, Anna."

Anna gave her a thumbs-up, doing her very best not to puke on Rosario's brown hiking boots.

"Where did you find the Hot Foot Powder?" Anna heard Taileybones ask.

"Believe it or not, we ran into the guy who invented Monsters and Mayhem."

"Really?"

"Yeah!" said Rosario excitedly. "Suvi was such a big fan that he gave us some of his, but by then the ritual had already finished and—yeah, obviously not great."

Anna sat back up, still drawing deep breaths as she stared at Rosario in disbelief. Her hood was back around her shoulders, but other than that, there was no sign she had just emerged from a room full of thousands of ghosts. In fact, she seemed to be positively glowing as she chatted with Taileybones.

Anna turned to Suvi, who looked like she'd been traveling in the Arctic, her face pale and her teeth chattering as she stared at Rosario in confusion.

Anna stood up, her knees still feeling more like Jell-O than joints.

"Rosario," said Anna. Her voice sounded hoarse, as if she'd been gargling with sandpaper.

"Yes?"

"How—how come the ghosts didn't affect you? You—" She looked Rosario up and down. "They didn't get you at all?"

Rosario shrugged casually, as if she took on armies of ghosts every day of the week. "They didn't bother me. I must be immune."

Anna furrowed her brow. It didn't make sense that the ghosts would impact her and Suvi but not Rosario.

"Did you find anything related to Billy?" Tailey-bones asked.

Rosario shook her head. "No one in the Order saw him pass through tonight, and none of the ghosts could sense him. He hasn't been here."

Anna's heart faltered. Her brain began to spiral at a dangerous speed. Okay, so Billy wasn't at the ritual. That didn't necessarily mean something bad had happened to him. He might've found someone else with Hot Foot Powder and continued after the witch, or he got sidetracked. He wasn't necessarily injured, and he wasn't necessarily dead.

Though she told herself this, Anna couldn't get the image of the ghosts out of her mind. She imagined a pale version of Billy lurking behind the bride with the hollow eyes, reaching out to touch her, his own face dripping with silver blood.

"Can I see the Hot Foot Powder?" Anna asked Rosario, holding her hands out to catch it.

Rosario nodded, tossing the ziplock bag to Anna.

Anna slid off her backpack and threw the powder in, before turning back to the rest of the group.

Anna sighed. "Guys, we need to hunt the Watcher."

"*What?*" Rosario asked.

"We need to hunt the Watcher," repeated Anna. "We know she's near the center of the forest. My family's encountered the Watcher there for centuries, but she always vanished before anyone could land a blow. Now we know she's been able to vanish because she uses Hot Foot Powder, but if we *also* use Hot Foot Powder, she won't be able to vanish from *our* sight. We can follow her. We can track her down."

Rosario shook her head. "That's not what we agreed—"

"I know it's not what we *agreed*," said Anna, nervously shifting from one foot to the other, "but everything's gotten way worse. Billy never made it to the Grand Ritual. We don't have the option of catching up with him anymore. He's already in enough danger with the cryptids, but if he gets cursed, he's as good as dead. If we kill the Watcher before midnight, we break the curse before it can impact Billy. We can give him a fighting chance to make it out of the forest."

Rosario sighed calmly, holding up a hand to silence Anna. "I know you're worried about Billy—we all are—

but being worried is no excuse for killing anyone. We need to focus on finding him, not taking on one of the most powerful witches in the history of the universe armed with nothing but a golf club."

"I've got kindling and a lighter."

"Do you actually think that will work against the Watcher?" Taileybones asked, unamused. "Kindling and a lighter? You saw the Not-Deer, right? That's one of her *servants*. How do you think your so-called weapons would work against the real deal?"

"It has to work," said Anna, embarrassment about her lack of equipment and ability burning her cheeks. "It's all I've got."

"We can try tracking him," offered Rosario. "You don't need to—"

"You don't *get* it!" shouted Anna, running a hand through her hair in frustration. "Billy's alone, he's going to be cursed at midnight, and I'm the only one who can save him! If he dies, it'll be my fault! He's going after the Watcher, so the next step for us has to be going after the Watcher. We might run into him along the way, but there's no point in wandering around the forest with no plan, just hoping he'll pop out of nowhere!"

Anna sighed shakily as she thought about the

incredible danger Billy was in. "I mean, what if it was one of *your* family members in trouble?"

Taileybones huffed, flicking his tail. "I see your point."

Rosario pursed her lips, turning from Taileybones to Anna. "Fine, then. We can try going after the Watcher, but if and when we do find her, we have to negotiate first—"

"The Watcher doesn't negotiate, though," said Anna nervously.

"How do you know she won't negotiate if you've never met her?"

"We *have* met her."

"I meant in person."

"I don't need to," said Anna. "My family's told me everything I need to know. It's all written down in Diligence's diary." Anna gestured to her backpack. "They may not know everything about other kinds of cryptids, but they haven't spent three hundred forty years hunting the Watcher and learned nothing. We need an attack plan, not a peace plan."

Taileybones glanced from Rosario to Anna. "I don't know . . ."

"Witches are evil monsters," said Anna sternly, ignoring Rosario's flinch. "That goes *double* for the Watcher.

I know you're into being peaceful with all of earth's creatures or whatever, but we can't take our chances trying to be nice to her. That's what Perseverance tried to do, and that's what got him killed."

"Were you there?" asked Rosario, her voice remarkably less cheerful than usual.

"I—huh?"

"Were you there when Perseverance Grimsbane was killed?"

"No?"

Rosario crossed her arms, staring determinedly up at Anna. "Then how do you know he tried to be nice?"

"Because my family doesn't lie?" said Anna. "What would they have to gain by lying about something like that?"

"Why would they lie about me?" asked Taileybones, a slight growl trembling in his throat. "You read what was written in the diary."

"It wasn't them who lied," Anna attempted to explain. "It was the guy who wrote to them about you."

"And then they wrote the lie down and let it justify their killing of hellhounds for the last ninety years."

Anna huffed. "Suvi, back me up here."

Silence answered.

"Suvi?"

There was still no response.

In the quiet, Anna could barely hear the forest singing.

> *The worms crawl in and the worms*
> *crawl out.*
> *The ones that go in are lean*
> *and thin.*
> *The ones that come out are fat*
> *and stout.*
> *Your eyes fall in and your teeth*
> *fall out.*

Anna furrowed her brow and turned. Suvi was still crouching on the forest floor. The tree's golden leaves skittered about her boots and filming equipment as she stared resolutely downward. Her dark hair shrouded her face, but Anna could see her shoulders shaking slightly.

"You all right?" asked Anna.

Suvi sat up and took a deep breath. Her brown eyes glistened, tears reflecting the moonlight as she looked to Taileybones.

"Are they all like that?" Suvi asked.

Anna turned from Suvi to Rosario and Taileybones, who seemed just as confused by Suvi's question as she was.

"What do you mean, Suvi?" asked Anna.

Suvi stood up, wrapping her arms around her middle as if protecting herself from something. "Are—are they all like that? Was—is he like that now?"

Anna's heart sank when she realized what Suvi was suggesting.

Mr. Kumar's death was unexpected, and it had not been easy on Suvi. Anna remembered Suvi's mom pulling her out of school for two weeks after the accident. She remembered Suvi and Mrs. Kumar standing next to the casket in the Grand Viewing Room as a sea of faceless people in white clothing shook their hands, the final thunk of the coffin closing on Mr. Kumar's ashen face before he went to the crematorium, so different from the smiling, cheerful man Anna knew.

Rosario sighed. "Suvi . . ."

"I thought they'd be different." Suvi took a deep breath through her nose. "I thought they'd be like how people are. I didn't think he'd be like that now."

"He's not!" said Anna, looking to Rosario and Taileybones for backup. "I mean, I'm sure he's not *really* like that. Dea—er, not living people—aren't supposed to be on our side of the veil. They get Ghost

197

Lurgy, just like we do. It messes with their heads, and they lose control of themselves. They probably aren't like that on the other side."

"Probably?" asked Suvi, throwing her hands up. Her cameras clanged metallically from the sudden movement. "That clears it all up, doesn't it? What happened to my dad! Where he went! How he's doing!"

"What happened to her dad?" Taileybones whispered.

"Use context clues," said Anna, waving him off.

"Like Taileybones and the Nain Rouge said, death is complicated," continued Rosario. "Humans can't really understand it."

"I—" Suvi looked down at her *Ghouligans* recording apparatus, a flush rising in her cheeks. "They were right all along. Neil and the bullies and everyone else online. *Ghouligans* is stupid. There was no point to any of it. Not the research. Not the videos. Not anything."

"Suvi, don't say that," said Taileybones. "From what you've told me, it's not stupid."

"Why would everyone in school make fun of *Ghouligans* if it wasn't stupid?" muttered Suvi, brushing away her tears furiously.

If possible, Anna's heart sank even lower. "Dude, you can't give in to them like that."

"You must still have Ghost Lurgy," said Rosario gently, reaching her hand out to Suvi. "Just sit back down—"

"I'm not going to sit back down!" Suvi shouted, wrenching herself away from Rosario. "I'm going home!"

Anna hesitated. She imagined Suvi walking home by herself in the thick darkness that surrounded them, her clinking cameras drawing the attention of every witch, ghost, and cryptid from Witchless to San Francisco.

"We're in the middle of the Watcher's forest," Taileybones attempted to explain. "It's Halloween night, and this place is crawling with cryptids who don't appreciate humans trespassing. Most aren't as patient as I am. Speaking as a cryptid, you can't go home."

"Why would I stay?" exclaimed Suvi angrily. "So I can run into my dad's ghost? So I can see him all bloody and crazy like the ghosts in there? Yeah, that sounds fun. Sounds like a *great* way to spend Halloween."

"If you leave now," said Anna, doing her very best to imitate Mom's business voice, "you'll get hurt or eaten or worse."

"I don't *care*!" screamed Suvi, her voice trembling. "I don't care anymore! Do you have *any* idea how bad it sucks to get made fun of every day, just because I want to talk to my dad again?"

The hush of the forest fell upon the clearing like rain upon a roof. None of them answered. They simply stared at Suvi in bewilderment.

"Do you know what it's like to have your things stolen and broken, all because people don't get you? They never leave me alone, no matter how many times I ask. They tell me I'm different and weird and nerdy, just because I'm trying to find a way to hug my dad again."

Suvi turned to Anna. "You said that we might run into ghosts tonight. I thought that I might *actually* see him. I thought that all of my hard work would finally pay off, but it was a huge waste of time. If my dad looks like *that*, then I don't want to see him. I certainly don't want to listen to the trees' *stupid* song anymore!"

"I get that you're upset," said Anna calmly. "I'd be upset if something happened to my dad too, but you can't go home—"

"Stop telling me what to do!" screamed Suvi. "*You're* the one always telling me to stick up for myself!"

"Not to *me*!" shouted Anna, immediately shaking her head at how ridiculous she sounded. "Look, I'm sorry people are mean to you at school, but I promise your dad isn't like those ghosts. You need to trust us."

Suvi shook her head. "No, I'm going . . ." Suvi furrowed her brow. "Taileybones, are you okay?"

Taileybones had gone rigid, staring straight at the tree line behind Suvi, his ears perked up like a German shepherd's. "Do you hear that?"

"Obviously not," said Anna, crossing her arms.

"Be quiet," growled Taileybones. His eyes followed the tree line as if following a mouse scampering along the floor. "It sounds like . . . running."

A sound like a whip echoed behind them. Anna found herself rocketing through the air. She landed on her stomach with a hard thump.

She grunted, then stood, rubbing her rib cage as she looked around.

She saw Rosario and Taileybones stand up, shaking their heads. Anna looked to her left and snapped to attention. "Where's Suvi?"

Rosario and Taileybones turned to look at the spot where Suvi had been moments before, their eyes growing wide with horror.

"Suvi!" Rosario yelled through cupped hands.

The forest was quiet. Not a single leaf moved. No branch broke. There was nothing but the sound of their breathing.

"Suvi!" Anna shouted.

There was no answer.

Suddenly a scream echoed through the forest.

Anna took off running, racing past her friends and bolting forward as quickly as she could go.

"SUVI!" she screamed. "SUVI!"

She broke into a small clearing and saw Suvi lying in the middle of the ground, unconscious. Her mutilated camera gear surrounded her like a mess of animal bones. Anna ran forward and reached out.

"ANNA, STOP!" Taileybones screamed.

The second Anna touched Suvi, another snap echoed through the forest. Anna's vision flashed white. Something knocked her off her feet.

A long-fingered hand closed around her ankle.

"Lights out," a voice rasped, just before the world went black.

17

Stretched and Starving

Fifty Minutes until Midnight

Anna woke up with a start and choked on the gag in her mouth. The darkness was thick, daunting, and stifling. She took a deep, heavy breath through her nose, trying to grasp her surroundings.

She was sitting in a spindly, stiff-backed wooden chair in a room that emanated a stench so strong and metallic, it felt like a handful of pennies had been stuffed up her nose.

Anna attempted to stand, but two thick ropes tied around her wrists held her tight to the tottering chair.

A door creaked open behind her. Anna's breath caught in her throat.

She was no longer alone.

Slow, dragging footsteps accompanied by distinct, heavy breathing grew closer, closer, and closer. She strained her neck to see who or what it could be. Her heart thudded as if attempting to leap from her chest and into the darkness.

Don't freak out. Don't freak out. Don't freak out.

Anna strained against the bonds again, but they simply wouldn't budge.

The footsteps stopped beside her, but the breathing did not.

Anna could see something watching her through the darkness. The form was barely blacker than the blackness surrounding it. It stood perfectly still, with its arms at its side. Its great, stretching hands splayed out like starfish. Whatever the form was, it was not a human. It was far too long for that.

Anna tried to steady herself. She wasn't going to let it know she was afraid. She was a Grimsbane, and she intended to act like one.

The form reached toward its hip. A flashlight flicked on, and Anna jumped in her seat.

A towering skeleton of a creature with needlelike yellow teeth stood over her. Its pale face was thin and sallow, the skin pulled tight over its skull as if a size too small for it. Its eyes were a fluorescent shade of red that blazed in the thin beam of light. Tattered camouflage clothing hung off the cryptid's emaciated frame like drapes over an open window. It smiled at Anna, blood dripping from the corner of its mouth.

It was a White Screamer.

She'd been captured by a White Screamer.

She was going to die.

Anna stared with wide, fearful eyes as the cryptid spun the flashlight in its hand.

"Let's get a better look at you, shall we?" The White Screamer's voice rasped like two pieces of metal rubbing together. It thrust the flashlight toward Anna's face and examined her hungrily, a manic gleam glowing in its flickering eyes. It reached a long, bony hand out and stroked Anna's cheek.

Anna jerked her head away.

The White Screamer tutted and seized a fistful of Anna's hair, forcing her to look up at its horrific face. Its expression was confusing. Behind the teeth and the blood . . . was that fear?

Anna tried to force herself out of the White Screamer's grasp, jerking her head to the side.

The White Screamer only chuckled and tightened its grip, yanking a few hairs from Anna's scalp. "I can already imagine the taste of your heart. The smell of the blood rushing through your veins." The White Screamer smiled with its horrible angler-fish teeth, blood weaving between them like water between dock posts. "I know you're afraid." It leaned down closer to Anna and whispered in a voice quieter than the light it was holding, "You should be—NO!"

The White Screamer shrieked—its voice suddenly more human than monster—and let go of Anna, taking a step back and hitting itself on the head. "NO! NO! NO! You don't *want* to hurt people! That's why you're so far out here! Oh God, why are they out here?"

Anna pulled against the restraints with as much force as she could muster. They simply wouldn't budge.

The White Screamer removed Anna's gag, settling it limply around her neck. "I'm sorry. I didn't mean to gag you. I just—I don't know what to do. I don't know what to do. I don't want to hurt you."

"It's—" Anna gulped, staring up at the terrifying creature's terrified eyes. The White Screamer didn't want to hurt Anna, but it didn't seem to be able to control its actions. "It's okay. You don't have to hurt me, but—" Anna's words got caught in her mouth. "Did you bring my friends here?" Anna had a horrible thought. "Did you . . . did you run into a boy earlier?"

"A boy?" mused the White Screamer as it stared at Anna, enthralled. "Is it possible I missed one when I picked you girls up? I haven't seen a human in nearly fifty years. I've been stuck eating animals—deer, rabbits, squirrels. I try not to eat people, but I can't help it." It smiled. "It's my nature to hunt them—to tear them apart—to feel their delicious, red blood run down my throat and into my stomach."

Anna's thoughts snapped to Suvi, Rosario, and Taileybones. "Where are my friends?"

"Oh, they're just fine," the White Screamer growled. "Aren't you, girls?"

It grabbed the armrest of Anna's chair and spun her around.

Suvi and Rosario were tied to chairs similar to hers. Rosario's hair was tussled, and Suvi had a nasty bruise on the side of her cheek, but other than that they seemed fine, albeit terrified as they pulled against their bonds.

"We've talked about struggling," sang the White Screamer softly as it slowly stalked toward them, its long, bare feet dragging against the carpeted floor. "I'm not planning on eating you three just yet, but I may just slip up if you keep misbehaving." A smile curled across the White Screamer's horrible face as it leaned close to Suvi, its head just inches from hers. "If you three misbehave, I'll eat the little one first."

"Leave her alone!" shouted Anna, trying with every ounce of strength she had to stand up. The way the White Screamer said "eat" made Anna's skin crawl. She didn't want the White Screamer getting anywhere near Suvi and Rosario.

"Do you want to get ripped apart?" the White Screamer asked Suvi, as if Anna hadn't spoken.

Suvi shook her head ferociously, her eyes wide and fearful.

The White Screamer smiled, reaching down with its long-fingered hand.

Its hand stopped just inches from her cheek, shaking. "I'm sorry."

The White Screamer wrenched its hand back and grabbed its head, throwing itself against the wall. "I'm sorry! I'm sorry! I'm sorry!" The White Screamer's flashlight fell to the floor. "I can't be here. I'll stop this. I can't—" It screeched in agony—a horrible sound that rattled Anna's skull. She'd never heard someone in so much pain in her life. The White Screamer fell to its knees. "I *can't* stop this!" It shrieked again, lurching forward. It scrambled to the door on all fours, skittering like a beetle. It gave a great wail of pain, slamming the door shut behind itself, leaving the girls alone.

Until it was gone, Anna didn't realize how fast and heavy her breaths were. She tried to steady her breathing. She had to stay calm. She could only figure a way out of this if she stayed calm.

"You all right?" Anna asked her friends, her voice barely above a mumble.

It was a stupid question, she knew, but Suvi and Rosario nodded. They looked as scared as Anna felt.

White Screamers were among the first cryptids she'd learned about as a kid—shrieking monsters that tore humans apart for fun, then ate them afterward. White Screamers were insanely intelligent and inhumanly quick, and had an insatiable desire to consume human flesh. Most people who tried to hunt them never came home, and their bodies were never found. It got so bad the Knights of Van Tassel banned White Screamer hunting in 1907. As far as Anna knew, no living hunter had come into contact with one since.

Now Anna, Suvi, and Rosario were stuck in a White Screamer's lair, and Taileybones was nowhere to be found. No matter how much the White Screamer didn't want to eat them, it apparently had no control over itself. It had taken up refuge far into the forest to avoid people, and they had walked right into its path.

Anna had to get her friends out of here, but escaping was an impossible task. Still, Anna had to try.

Anna looked down at her spindly wooden chair and shook it. It wobbled from side to side, creaking a bit. It was weak. The wooden floor was not. Anna considered this for a moment.

This would have to work. She would only have one chance.

Anna took a deep breath, then kicked up as hard as she could.

The chair fell backward and shattered on the floor.

Anna stood up and ripped the straggling bits of wood and rope away from her wrists.

She turned to her friends, held a finger to her lips, then pointed to the door. They sat in silence for a moment, waiting for a sign that the White Screamer had heard Anna break from her bonds. All Anna could hear was the wind whistling outside and the unmistakable sound of rustling trees, but no White Screamer.

Anna turned purposefully to Suvi. She took the gag off her friend's mouth and began untying her ropes.

"Do you hear it?" Anna whispered.

"No," answered Suvi, barely audible.

Anna finished untying Suvi's right hand. She set to freeing Rosario while Suvi worked to free her left.

Anna took the gag off Rosario's mouth.

"You all right?" Anna asked.

"I could be better," Rosario muttered. Her hand flicked upward, gesturing to a purple, golf ball–sized bruise blossoming on her forehead.

"Fair enough." Anna continued with Rosario's bonds. Suvi got up to assist.

"Taileybones?" Suvi asked.

Anna and Rosario shook their heads.

Anna grimaced. She didn't know if White Screamers targeted other cryptids. The possibility that the White Screamer had Taileybones trapped in some other room all by himself made her heart twist. Anna thought about how nice Taileybones had been at the Grand Ritual and remembered him taking a stand with them against the melonheads. Taileybones had been with the team every step of the way.

Anna couldn't leave without him.

Anna finally got Rosario's left hand free. She and Suvi helped her to her feet.

"All right," whispered Anna. "I know this is a bad situation, but we need to stay calm and find Taileybones. We can't leave without him. Agreed?"

Suvi and Rosario nodded.

Anna steeled her heart for what she had to do next.

"The only way to find him is to take a look around, and to take a look around, I'm going to have to open the door."

"I'll do it," said Rosario instantly.

Anna shook her head. "I'm the one who made us go on the hunt in the first place, and I've got more experience than both of you, even if it's limited. You guys have to promise to follow my lead."

Suvi nodded determinedly. Rosario didn't respond.

"Rosario?" asked Anna.

Rosario sighed but gave her a half-hearted thumbs-up. Under the present circumstances, that was good enough for Anna.

She brushed past Suvi and Rosario to the exit, moving as quietly as possible. Anna took the cold, tarnished doorknob in her hand, holding it as lightly as she could. She closed her eyes and slowly—*slowly*—opened the door.

CREEEEAAAAAAAK!

The noise ripped through the silence.

Anna retreated back into the room and pressed herself against the wall. Her heart thumped wildly against her chest like a trapped animal. She counted to ten . . . to twenty . . . to thirty . . . waiting to hear a shriek, but it never came.

The White Screamer hadn't heard them.

"C'mon," she whispered to Suvi and Rosario, gesturing to the door.

"Maybe I should go first," Rosario whispered.

"Why would you go first?"

"Um . . ." Rosario scrunched up her nose. "I just—I just think it might be better if you were in the back. That way nothing could sneak up on us."

Anna shook her head. "That makes no sense. You guard the rear. I'll stay up front. Just follow me."

"Are you sure?"

Anna paused, staring at Rosario in confusion. "Do you not trust me or something?"

Rosario shook her head. "No, no. I didn't mean it like that. I was just thinking of other options. You go first."

"All right, then," said Anna, still a bit confused by Rosario's desire to be in front. "Everyone, stay quiet."

Slowly, Anna led Suvi and Rosario out of the room.

It took Anna's eyes a few moments to adjust to the darkness. The basement ahead of them was almost as long as the funeral home's Grand Viewing Room. A single lamp at the end cast a ghostly orange light on the dilapidated furniture, peeling seventies-style wallpaper, and the sinking wooden staircase at the end of the room.

"Abandoned hunting cabin," muttered Suvi, letting out a despondent groan. "Super."

Anna stared in horror at a large brown stain that seemed permanently melded into the wooden floor. She tried not to think too hard about what it meant.

"Anna, is this yours?" whispered Rosario.

Anna turned and saw Rosario gesture to her backpack, thrown carelessly onto a decrepit orange couch. Anna sighed in relief and slung it onto her back. Madeline would've killed her if she'd lost Diligence's diary to a White Screamer. Her golf club was still lodged firmly in the backpack, sticking out the top. The White Screamer hadn't been able to touch the iron. She removed it and held it tightly with both hands.

Anna continued onward, listening carefully for the dragging of the White Screamer's feet.

The door at the top of the stairs opened to reveal a dimly lit hallway. Creeping down, they finally reached a sitting room illuminated only by the moonlight peeking through the windows. Anna did her best to slowly and quietly lead Suvi and Rosario through the house, stepping over old, beat-up furniture that looked like it had been deposited by a tornado. She kept an eye out for any sign of Taileybones, all while trying to ignore the horrific sounds overwhelming the cabin. The White Screamer was howling in pain—a horrible, aching, gut-wrenching sound that made Anna's heart twist into knots.

"I CAN'T KILL THEM!" the White Screamer cried. "I WON'T KILL THEM! I WON'T!"

"Do you hear that?" Rosario whispered.

"I hear it," Anna muttered. "I don't want to, but I do."

"Not *that*," said Rosario, nodding to the door on the other side of the room. "Listen."

Anna turned.

There, just barely audible under the horrific yelling echoing throughout the house, was a faint scratch, scratch, scratch against the frame of the door leading outside—the sound of strong claws trying to break through the door and into the cabin as quietly as possible. Anna recalled a line from Diligence's diary.

The night of Townsend's death, Sikes witnessed a creature we Grimsbanes know to be a hellhound crawl out of a hole it clawed in Townsend's cabin wall.

"Taileybones," muttered Anna, a flood of relief washing over her.

She slowly turned to look at Suvi and Rosario, who

were staring at her with wide, knowing eyes.

Quietly, Anna, Suvi, and Rosario moved as carefully and quickly as they could through the living room, tiptoeing across the floor toward the door. Anna held her breath, cautiously avoiding the broken furniture and glass scattered upon the floor. It was like stepping around land mines. They were just feet away from the door—feet away from escaping!

Anna heard a snap and spun.

Before she could swing her golf club, the White Screamer's hands were on her coat.

It pulled her off the floor. She dangled hopelessly in the air, the White Screamer's pointed teeth a pencil's length from her nose.

"LET HER GO!" Suvi yelled.

The White Screamer lurched forward and dropped Anna. Suvi was off the floor now. She had jumped onto the White Screamer's back and was beating it on the head with her fist, like an incredibly deadly backpack.

The White Screamer grabbed Suvi's arms and flung her forward over its head. She slammed into the floor and wheezed, grabbing her chest.

"Cute try, sweetie, but that won't stop me from killing her," said the White Screamer as it looked down at

Suvi, its clawed hand raised. "It certainly won't stop me from killing you—"

Anna charged the White Screamer like a football player, grabbing it by the knees and knocking it back to the floor.

The White Screamer kicked and Anna flew backward, landing painfully on top of Suvi.

The White Screamer stood up. It towered over them, pale and horrible in the faint gleam of the lamp. Blood dripped off its teeth like red candle wax, dribbling down its chin and onto its skeletal chest.

"I don't want to do this," it growled through gritted teeth, "but no one's ever escaped." It raised a hideous, clawed hand into the air. "You can't escape."

"Correction," said Rosario.

Anna's jaw dropped.

Rosario stood confidently with her hands on her hips, staring at the White Screamer like a vengeful, pink-coated goddess. "They'll never escape without me."

Like a light turning on, the air began to shift. It was as if the particles had collectively agreed to stop moving and stand at attention. The air buzzed with a definite energy, ready to charge at the nearest object it was pointed at.

Rosario raised her right hand.

The air raced toward her, rippling in her direction like waves about to crash on a shore.

Rosario made a fist and punched outward.

The wind whistled and flew at the White Screamer. It staggered backward. Anna grabbed Suvi and yanked her out of the way.

"WITCH!" shrieked the White Screamer.

Rosario raised her hands again. The darkness in her eyes expanded to fill the whites. Her curls glided upward, as if she were suspended in water.

Rosario smiled.

"I prefer the term lechuza."

18

An Oncoming Storm

Forty Minutes until Midnight

The White Screamer roared and ran at Rosario.

Rosario was ready. She held her hands up and sent another burst of air at the creature, knocking it off its feet.

"THE DOOR!" shouted Rosario, preparing another charge with her hands. "GO!"

Anna was too shocked to move, seemingly glued to the floor as she stared at Rosario in her new, witchy state.

"Anna, c'mon!" screamed Suvi, grabbing Anna's arm and lifting her off the floor.

Suvi's voice pulled Anna back to reality. She picked her golf club up, raced to the door, and wrenched it open, letting in a blast of freezing fall air. She heard the White Screamer shriek and turned back.

"GO!" shouted Suvi, shoving her out the door.

Anna stumbled backward down the stairs and landed with a dull thud on something soft.

"You're okay!" Anna shouted, stepping away from Taileybones. His wolfish face was racked with concern.

"Where's Rosario?" he asked, staring in horror from Anna and Suvi to the cabin. "It's a White Screamer. I've been clawing my way in—"

"ROSARIO, C'MON!" screamed Suvi desperately, staring despairingly into the endless darkness of the entranceway.

Just then, Rosario hurtled out of the door. She stumbled onto the dirt and fell to her knees.

Anna, Suvi, and Taileybones rushed forward to help.

"Run!" Rosario shouted as she staggered to her feet, starting to run toward the forest. "Go!"

They didn't need her to tell them twice. Anna sprinted away, racing through the trees with Suvi and Taileybones beside her.

A great gust of air launched Anna off her feet. She landed painfully on her stomach. The intense, howling wind lashed at her hair as she looked about. Twigs and leaves rocketed past her. A huge branch nearly struck Anna in the face.

Anna rolled over and saw Rosario standing in the middle of the tempest, but she looked very unlike herself. She was standing taller. Energy seemed to rush into her hands from the air around them as she held them above her head, moving them in a circular motion.

A gigantic mass of rolling black clouds gathered above the cabin. They rotated about the roof, crackling with thin bursts of lightning.

"COVER YOUR HEADS!" Anna heard Taileybones scream.

Rosario let out an ear-shattering scream, leapt up, and brought her hands against the earth.

BOOOOOOOOOOOOOOM!

The biggest lightning bolt Anna had ever seen struck the ground between them and the cabin. It surged through the earth with tremendous speed. Anna watched as Rosario maneuvered her hands inward. The earth splintered, snapping and folding into itself as an enormous canyon at least thirty feet wide opened around the cabin, encircling it. The cabin began to crumble as thunder roiled above them. Anna heard a distant shriek—the White Screamer, surely stuck inside the house as it tumbled downward. Soon, Anna couldn't even hear the White Screamer shrieking over the roar of the wind and thunder.

Eventually, Rosario lifted her hands. The wind stopped, and the clouds dissipated.

Anna ran a hand through her tangled hair, staggering to her feet. Her mouth tasted like metal. The hair on her arms stood straight up.

Where the horrific cabin had once been, there was only a demolished pile of wood, plaster, and stone surrounded by a massive crater.

Rosario calmly rose to her feet, dusted herself off, and strolled back toward the group.

Anna turned to Suvi and Taileybones. Suvi stared at Rosario with an open mouth and wide eyes, a blend of fear and shock. Taileybones didn't seem even moderately surprised. He was instead focusing intently on Anna and Suvi.

"Are you all right?" he asked.

"Yes," said Suvi in a small voice, looking around Rosario back at the space where the cabin once stood. "Um—what was—"

"I don't know," answered Rosario, scowling at the destruction as if unsure if she'd caused it. "I just . . . I didn't want to take any chances. The White Screamer was about to kill you guys."

Rosario walked to Suvi and Taileybones and sat down. Anna, not knowing what else to do, and trying to gather her thoughts, did the same.

For a long while, they just sat there in silence, trying to catch their breath.

Despite having a clear view of the hole that had undoubtedly trapped the White Screamer, Anna didn't feel safe. She kept thinking about the cryptid, with its red eyes and needlelike teeth, its hungry grin and the blood dripping from its face, the way it cried out in pain because it didn't want to kill them.

She shuddered.

Everyone else seemed just as shell-shocked. They sat on the forest floor, not speaking, not even looking at one another.

"How are you feeling, Suvi?" asked Taileybones after a moment.

"Hard to say," said Suvi, still gazing hollowly at the ruined cabin from her seated position. "On one hand, I've been right about White Screamers existing all along. On the other, I almost got eaten by one and lost all my *Ghouligans* footage."

Taileybones nodded sympathetically. "It happens to the best of us."

Suvi sighed, turning to Rosario and Anna. "I'm sorry I yelled at you guys. The trees' song was driving me nuts, and I just got upset, y'know, with my dad and stuff. I shouldn't have taken my issues out on you, and I should've been more honest." Suvi took a deep breath. "When Anna said she wanted to look for Billy, I thought we might also find my dad. It wasn't right to not tell you guys my reasons for coming." She smiled at Rosario. "It's pretty cool you're a witch."

"Lechuza, actually, but bruja is fine also," said Rosario. "The terms better reflect my spiritual lineage and the roots of my magical abilities." She brushed cabin dust off her coat. "Thanks, though. I think being a lechuza is pretty cool too."

Anna felt a sinking sensation in her stomach as she stared at Rosario. She remembered Rosario's eyes growing black, her hair floating, the sheer power she'd wielded against the White Screamer. Anna recalled how Rosario had been unaffected by the ghosts, undoubtedly an ability she had because she was a witch.

Even though Rosario's abilities were helpful, they felt wrong. Witches—lechuzas—were supposed to be monsters.

Anna wasn't sure she agreed with Suvi about Rosario.

"How—how long have you been a lechuza for?" asked Anna cautiously.

Rosario shrugged, moving to sit cross-legged. "Since I was born. I wanted to tell you, but your family's pretty anti-bruja and my moms wouldn't let me—"

"Your moms are witches? Er, brujas?" Anna noticed Taileybones shift uncomfortably, almost like he was getting ready to jump.

Rosario nodded proudly. "My entire family has had powers since birth. My moms adopt orphaned witches. Everyone practices brujería in some sense, but we all have different specializations. Salvador and I are lechuzas, so we can make storms, and one day, if we really practice, we should be able to turn into giant owls. My moms are psychics. Xander can make illusions—"

"Can you undo curses?" Anna blurted, staring expectantly at Rosario.

Rosario recoiled. "I—I'm sorry, what?"

"Can you undo curses?" asked Anna, hope fluttering her heart. "Like, the Grimsbane family curse?"

"Oh." Rosario's brow furrowed as she shook her head. "Oh, no, that's not how curses work."

Anna felt the hope that had built so rapidly inside her pop like a balloon. "Course you can't."

"What's that supposed to mean?"

"I don't know," muttered Anna, trying to ignore the tugging in her heart, which seemed to be working its way to her eyes. "I mean, you're a lechuza, right? A witch? So—"

Anna hesitated.

"So what?" asked Rosario, a concerned expression crossing her face.

Anna sighed. "Are you, like, on board with the whole cursing-people thing? Or the eating-people thing?"

"I'm not," said Rosario definitively. "Witches don't *actually* eat people. That's a myth. Most witches don't even curse people. I'm obviously not a fan of that, nor is anyone else in my family."

Anna knew this made sense, on some level. Anna thought back to eating breakfasts with Billy, Suvi, and Rosario at the Blue Moon, to the sleepovers and the *Vampires of West Grove High* movie nights. She thought back to her interactions with members of Rosario's family. Rosario was one of Anna's best friends. The Ortiz-Riveras had lived across the street from the Grimsbanes for as long as Anna could remember. Anna knew they were good people.

Despite this, Anna couldn't help recalling everything her family had taught her about witches. She thought about the flash cards she spent hours studying and the witch-hunter posters in her bedroom. She remembered the witches and cryptids whose misdeeds were detailed in Diligence's diary. She thought about the untimely deaths of a plethora of family members—struck down by the curse, or killed on a particularly deadly hunt. Anna knew that witches were evil.

But then how could Rosario be a witch?

Anna sighed as she stood up, running a hand through her hair. "You—you've been lying about being a witch this whole time, Rosario."

Rosario moved to stand with Anna. "I've been lying to keep my family safe."

"From what?"

"From *your family*."

Anna faltered. Taileybones and Suvi exchanged worried glances but didn't say anything.

"What do you mean, safe from my family?"

"You're witch hunters. We're brujas," said Rosario, as if this were enough to explain hiding the biggest secret in the history of secrets. She shifted from her left foot to her right, wringing her hands nervously. "I mean, you guys typically stick to witches who make trouble, but brujería's not exactly something we can advertise with the Indiana branch of the Knights of Van Tassel living across the street."

Anna opened her mouth and closed it, unsure how to respond.

Would her family hunt Rosario's family if they knew they were brujas?

"We're not like that," said Anna in an authoritative voice. "We take calls from people who are being hurt by witches, ghosts, and cryptids. We *help* people."

"It's not up to you to decide who does and does not count as people," interjected Taileybones, his red eyes narrowing at Anna as he stepped protectively toward Rosario. "Hunters, witches, cryptids . . . what's the difference? We're all the same."

Anna shook her head. "Witches and cryptids hurt people—"

"So do hunters," retorted Taileybones. "You read Diligence's diary. You've seen the lies they wrote—"

"You want to talk about *lying*?" Anna snapped. "I'm not the liar here! Rosario's been lying as long as we've known her!"

"She's lied for good reasons, though," interjected Suvi, standing next to Taileybones and Rosario. "I mean, your family *hunts* witches and cryptids and stuff! You don't talk to them or try to make friends with them, you just kill them! I'd be quiet if I was a lechuza too, if your mom might kill my mom."

"Thanks," Rosario muttered.

"No problem."

"So, you're siding with Rosario, then?" Anna asked, the tugging in her heart getting stronger with Suvi's betrayal.

"I'm not siding with anyone," corrected Suvi, holding up her hands defensively. "I'm just trying to explain Rosario's point of view."

Anna shook her head, a well of confusion filling her brain as she studied her friends. The back of her eyes began to sting painfully. "My family's not bad, though. The Watcher cursed us."

"I don't think it was random," said Rosario plainly. "Witches don't just throw curses around, especially not curses as powerful as your family's. The Watcher was likely provoked."

"It's not my family's fault we were cursed!" Anna protested, her vision becoming slightly watery as she held tears back, trying to look stronger than she felt. "Why are you siding with the Watcher?"

"Because it might just be a misunderstanding!"

"You're *actually* siding with an evil witch over me?"

"I'm not!"

"You think my family *deserved* to be cursed?" shouted Anna. "That Billy and my dad and cousins and uncles might deserve to die? Just because the Watcher might've misunderstood something?"

"No one said anyone deserves to die," Rosario said calmly. "Let's just take a deep breath—"

"I'm not going to take a deep breath!" screamed Anna.

Her friends fell silent.

"I don't understand," Anna said quietly, wiping at her eyes with the back of her hand. "I don't get this at all."

"I'm still me," Rosario said, her voice shaking. "Anna, I promise, I'm no different—"

"But you *are*!" exclaimed Anna.

Taileybones growled, and Suvi gasped. Taileybones was staring at Anna with the utmost disgust, as if this whole situation were somehow Anna's fault.

As if *she'd* been the one lying to her friends for years.

"I'm not different!" shouted Rosario, tears beginning to glisten in her dark eyes. "I'm exactly the same."

"You aren't the same! You're a witch!" yelled Anna, stepping backward. "You've been buddy-buddy with

230

the cryptids this whole time. You've been lying since I first met you! You use magic, and now I can't tell if you're lying!"

"About what?"

"About the Watcher!" shouted Anna. "About whether or not you're siding with her and going to turn on us once we get there!"

"Hey," warned Taileybones. "That's not fair—"

"None of this is fair!" screamed Anna. "Billy's missing! He could be dead! It's up to me to save him, and now everyone's siding against me!"

"We still want to help you find him," said Taileybones, "but there's a better way."

Anna stared at Taileybones and Rosario, her thoughts hardening like ice in her mind. Taileybones had known about Rosario's powers this whole time. They'd both lied to her.

"I don't—I don't think I want your help," Anna said quietly.

Rosario stepped forward, reaching out a hand. "Anna—"

"I'm serious." Anna stepped back, tears now falling freely down her face. "I can't . . . I can't trust you. I'm sorry, but I can't. Not with Billy depending on me."

Rosario's face was wrought with hurt as she took

her hand back, nearly running into Suvi. Suvi put a supportive hand on Rosario's shoulder. It felt like a knife in Anna's heart.

Taileybones simply sat and shook his head. "Just when I thought a hunter might be different, you had to prove me wrong."

The knife in Anna's heart twisted even more, but she didn't have time to pay attention to it. She had to find Billy.

Anna turned to Suvi. "Are you coming?"

"What?"

"Are you coming, or are you staying?"

Suvi looked from Anna to Rosario, then back to Anna. "Anna, I can't just—"

"Fine," said Anna, steeling herself as she slid her golf club back into her backpack. "You made your choice."

Anna wiped the tears from her eyes, turned around, and continued straight and soldierlike into the forest, ignoring her friends' shouts behind her. She checked her watch—just thirty minutes until midnight.

Anna was going to save Billy, and she certainly didn't need the help of a lechuza to do so.

19

Phantom Fingers

Fifteen Minutes until Midnight

The forest was much worse when Anna was by herself.

She marched slowly, her teeth chattering and her breath coming out in white puffs as she continued along the narrow pathway. All around her the trees seemed to move and shift, turning to one another and pointing at the pathetic little girl all alone in the dark forest beneath their constant, incessant singing.

Don't you laugh when the hearse
goes by
'Cause you might be the next to die.

233

They'll wrap you up in a clean
white sheet
And put you down about six
feet deep.

It was like something out of the fairy tales Dad used to read to her, Madeline, and Billy when they were little, about kids who got lost in the woods, only to be preyed upon by witches and monsters.

Anna felt her eyes getting hot at the memory and quickly shoved it away. There was no time to focus on that. She had to save Billy.

Anna continued forward. The dead leaves and mud mushed beneath her tennis shoes as she listened intently, both for Billy and anything that may have been lurking in the hundreds of shadows cast by the moonlight. She kept her flashlight pointed at the ground, scanning the path for any sign of her brother—a footprint, a glove. Anything that could point her in his direction.

The worst part about being alone was that it gave Anna plenty of time to think.

She'd left Rosario, Suvi, and Taileybones. Rosario was a witch. No, not a witch—a lechuza. Rosario said she and her family didn't do evil things, but if that was true, then why would they keep their magic a secret? Anna's family hunted witches, but she didn't think they'd ever hunt Rosario's family.

Would they?

Anna racked her brain, trying to remember a time any of her family members spoke about hesitating before killing a witch or cryptid. If there'd been an incident like that, Anna couldn't recall. The number one rule of hunting was to instantly engage, incapacitate, and kill. That was the family motto—emblazoned above the basement door, on the cover of Diligence's diary. So did that mean the Grimsbanes would engage, incapacitate, and kill Rosario if they knew she was a lechuza? Or engage, incapacitate, and kill Taileybones without hearing his side of the story?

Anna thought back to the sharp *thwip* of Madeline's crossbow as an arrow shot through a straw dummy, the scent of fire that always seemed to linger in the basement, and the all too familiar laughter that seemed to drift up the stairs whenever the women were training.

Did her family think hunting witches and cryptids was funny?

Anna shook her head. No. No, they didn't. The Grimsbane women hunted because they had to. They had to save the Grimsbane men and other people who needed protection from witches and ghosts and cryptids.

Now the person most in need of protection from witches and cryptids was Billy. Anna didn't have time to think about her problems when he could be hurt and alone. She hadn't seen so much as a blink of him since the Nain Rouge. She checked her watch. There were only fifteen minutes until midnight. Fifteen minutes until her and Billy's thirteenth birthday. Fifteen minutes until Billy got cursed to die a horrible, miserable death while in a forest surrounded by cryptids.

If Anna was being honest, it wasn't looking great.

This was all Anna's fault. She wasn't an experienced witch hunter. She should've called Mom and waited for her to get home. That way, her aunts and cousins could've rescued Billy and brought him back. If she'd done that, Billy would be safe, she'd still have her friends, and she could've avoided this whole big mess. Anna couldn't believe how badly she'd screwed this up.

Something hit Anna straight in the stomach, pulling her out of her thoughts. She fell forward, clutching an object as she righted herself.

It was only upon standing upright that Anna realized there was nothing in front of her.

The trees' song stopped.

Anna furrowed her brow, turning behind her to see if she could've possibly tripped, but the path was just as empty as it had been when she trod upon it seconds ago. Anna stared into the space illuminated by her flashlight beam, feeling wholeheartedly confused.

She'd just hit something solid. The dull pain in her middle was evidence of that. She'd also used something to stand up, but there wasn't anything on the path but her.

Anna turned back around and reached out. Her hand brushed against something.

Anna withdrew as if it had burned her.

Her hand had touched something invisible.

She took off her glove and felt it again, stroking the object's splintery, wooden surface, solid beneath her touch. Whatever it was, it was clear that someone or something didn't want her to see it.

Luckily, Anna had just the solution.

Anna removed the Hot Foot Powder from her backpack and opened the ziplock bag. She reached in and grabbed a pinch between her thumb and forefinger before putting her backpack back on.

It was only then that Anna realized she didn't know how to use Hot Foot Powder. Was she supposed to swallow it? Inhale it? Sprinkle it on herself?

Anna wrinkled her nose and sniffed it. The stench hit her like a cannonball. She gagged.

Sprinkling it on herself it was. If that didn't work, she'd take a more desperate approach.

Anna took a deep breath and closed her eyes. She held the pinch of Hot Foot Powder over her head, sprinkled it, and opened her eyes.

At first she thought it hadn't worked. Then the dirt in front of her began to shift.

Anna yelped and leapt back as the earth reached its way upward. The squelching, gurgling mud twisted into a thin column, spreading out as it reached a longer, rectangular portion of the object. The dirt fell back to the earth and shot off in the direction Anna had been walking in.

The sign was ancient. The wood was rotting and decaying. Despite this, it stood proudly in the ground as if it had sprouted legs and chosen the spot all for itself. It reminded Anna of old Great-Uncle Monty seated in his favorite squashed-up armchair.

Anna noticed there was writing engraved on the front of it. She shone her flashlight on the sign, kneeling to examine the barely visible letters closely.

"'Witchless, New Cornwallshire,'" she muttered aloud, tracing the letters with her right hand. "'Population: Four. Trespassers will be shot.'"

Anna squinted and leaned forward, examining the lettering more closely. A number two had originally been written to denote the population, but it was crossed out and replaced with a three, then a four. The handwriting on the numbers was remarkably familiar.

Anna heard a snap.

Her head shot up like a prairie dog's.

The shadows the flashlight beam created stood tall and menacing in the silence, punctuated only by the few rustling leaves high above her and the whispering of the trees, ever present, observing the forest with their all-seeing eyes.

The forest appeared empty.

"Billy?" Anna whispered.

She heard a crashing thud on the path behind her and turned.

The Not-Deer lay in a heap upon the ground. Every limb in its body was contorted at an impossible angle, every joint dislocated—a hastily assembled pile of barely attached body parts. For a moment, Anna assumed it was dead, but then its head began to move. Slowly, impossibly, the head rotated, swiveling upward to look at Anna. It smiled at her with its too-wide grin.

"I told you your friends were keeping secrets," the Not-Deer said.

Anna watched in horror as the Not-Deer's limbs cracked and turned, crunching as the mound of body parts that was the Not-Deer began shifting upward.

"Curious how you responded," rasped the Not-Deer as it re-formed. "Curious how you abandoned them after learning all you learned about us—about your own friend." The Not-Deer's eyes stared at Anna the entire time—glowing white and unfeeling. "Curious how you responded to the cryptids the Watcher sent your way this evening—how you committed to continuing your hunt despite all the opportunities you had to learn—the opportunities you had to repent. You've made some *very* bad decisions, but your choices demonstrate who you are, don't they?"

The Not-Deer towered over Anna. Its antlers stretched into the sky, its broad chest puffed out toward her. It took a confident step forward and bowed low, its smiling face barely a foot from hers. "You're a hunter, Anna Grimsbane, and the Watcher knows it."

A low, rumbling laugh echoed from behind Anna.

A chill shot down Anna's spine and pulled her out of her trance. She sprang into action, dropping her flashlight, grabbing her golf club, and pulling it out of her backpack. Anna held it beside her ear with both hands, ready to swing. She spun to look behind, but no one was there.

When she looked back to the Not-Deer, it was gone.

The forest settled into a heavy silence, weighing upon her like a thick overcoat. Anna turned about, looking for the source of the laughter, but there was nothing. It was just her, the sign, and the trees. Perhaps she'd imagined it.

"Little hunter, all alone?" hissed a hollow voice next to Anna's ear.

Anna swung the golf club as hard as she could. She hit nothing but air. The force of the swing dragged her forward.

Another laugh echoed through the forest.

Something tugged Anna's hair, yanking her head sharply against the nape of her neck. It disappeared as quickly as it appeared.

"So far from home," whispered the voice.

Something kicked the back of her knee. It buckled

and she staggered forward, clutching onto the "Witchless, New Cornwallshire" sign to keep from falling.

"All alone. All alone," the voice sang playfully, tugging painfully at Anna's hair.

Anna swung the golf club. Again, she swung through air.

Her heart hammered in her chest as she spun, looking for whatever was causing this. Wasn't the Hot Foot Powder supposed to let her see the Watcher? If this was the Watcher tormenting her, then why couldn't Anna see her? Had she used the Hot Foot Powder incorrectly?

"Nice try!" sang the voice, chuckling deeply.

Anna shouted in frustration and swung the golf club in an arc.

The rumbling laugh resounded again. "Oooh! You were closer that time. Your brother didn't get nearly as close."

Billy.

"I don't want any trouble," said Anna quickly. "I just want my brother."

Anna heard her own words echo back as if she were in a cave, replaying two, three, four times.

The leaves hissed with malice as the earth began to

rumble. The trees bent and shook, their trunks creaking with laughter as they ogled Anna standing alone in the forest at the mercy of an invisible tormenter. That's when the trees' branches began to lower toward her, forming grasping wooden hands as long and gnarled as a witch's.

Anna blanched as she realized it wasn't the Watcher that had been toying with her.

It was the forest itself.

"You just want your brother?" groaned a tree.

A branched hand shot out from the shadows, grabbed Anna's wrist, and twisted.

Anna watched in horror as its sharp, barky fingers dug into her skin, drawing droplets of blood that oozed from the crescent-shaped nail marks. The droplets traced down Anna's pale wrist and dropped to the forest floor, which absorbed them with an unnatural, thirsty fervor.

"Then why did you bring an iron weapon?" asked a tree behind her.

The grasp hardened. Anna tried to back away, but it only got impossibly tighter.

"Why is there kindling and lighter fluid in your bag?" asked a tree to her left.

The wooden hand twisted her wrist farther.

Anna yelped in pain and dropped the golf club.

The hand didn't let go. "No answer?"

Anna tried to wrench her wrist away, tears spilling out of her eyes as the pain crept up to her elbow. "Stop!"

The hand yanked Anna's wrist downward, forcing her to her knees before suddenly letting go.

Anna barely had time to gasp in pain and grab her wrist before two more hands grabbed hold of her hair, slamming her onto her back.

The trees began to drag Anna through the forest at an impossible speed, their roots reaching out of the ground to propel her backward. Anna screamed, desperately trying to plant her feet to slow the trees dragging her as twigs and branches scratched her face. It was no use. Her hand-me-down shoes scuttled helplessly over the leaves that lined the forest floor. She grasped the wet soil with her fingers, trying to dig her hands into the dirt and mud.

"STOP!" she screamed, reaching upward to scratch at the trees' hands. "STOP! PLEASE, STOP!"

The trees let go, and Anna scrambled forward.

A root shot out of the ground, grabbed her ankle, and yanked backward. Anna fell flat, hitting her chin on the ground.

"You know," a tree said harshly. "I really hate whiners."

Anna heard a soft rustle, a word spoken in a language she didn't understand, and felt a tremendous pressure behind her skull.

Before she could scream, the world snapped shut.

20

The Cottage

Anna woke up on a stiff wooden floor with a sick feeling in her stomach. Her brain felt like lead. For a moment, she lay there with her eyes closed, trying to recall how she had ended up on a wooden floor in the first place. The humid air clung to her skin like a wet beach towel. She could barely hear a faint crackling noise over the wind outside, leading her to believe there was some sort of fire nearby. She shifted slightly and felt her wrist sting.

Anna remembered what had happened.

The trees had grabbed her. They'd been trying to take her somewhere. Given the unfamiliarity of her surroundings, it seemed they had succeeded.

Anna kept her eyes closed and her breathing even despite the panic she felt rising in her chest. She listened closely to find out if there was someone or something with her, but she didn't hear movement.

Carefully Anna opened her eyes a fraction of an inch. It was still dark, but that could've meant anything. She could've been here three minutes or three days. Wherever here was.

She was in some sort of cottage—a cluttered, thatch-roofed hut with fingerlike plants weaving between the planked walls, creating large gaps through which moonlight shone on jars, cages, and shelves full of an assortment of materials: swimming tadpoles, leather-bound books with foreign words on the binding, sloshing liquids eager to escape their jars. To her left was an ancient dinner table surrounded by four chairs and a squashy, unmade bed. To her right was a cauldron and a roaring hearth. The fire emitted a supernaturally strong heat and cast a flickering orange glow upon the room.

Anna sat up and readjusted her backpack. She rubbed her bloodied wrist, wincing as she studied a jar full of marbles on the shelf in front of her. She leaned in toward it, examining the white spheres with increasing curiosity.

Something seemed . . . *off* about them.

Anna was about to pick up the jar when one of the marbles blinked.

Anna screamed and scrambled backward.

Eyes. The jar was full of living eyes.

Anna stumbled to her feet so quickly she knocked a bottle of frog hearts off a shelf. It fell to the floor and shattered. Anna turned about, desperately looking for an exit—a window or a door or something, but there was none.

She stopped spinning.

Anna was trapped.

"Finally awake?"

Anna jumped and turned to the table. A silver-haired woman in a floor-length black dress and cloak sat in the chair farthest from her, lounging among the horrific jarred ingredients as if they were not only to be expected, but also appreciated. She was tall and lean and beautiful in a way that called to mind aging actresses who drew the attention of any room they entered. Her pale skin glowed slightly, as if she were from another world. She examined Anna with lamp-like, yellow eyes.

The room was silent aside from the fire, the foreign sounds of the cottage, and Anna's heart thumping against her chest. The woman gave off the same ancient, electric energy as the Nain Rouge, only deeper, angrier, and far more powerful. She raised a thin eyebrow and turned her head slightly to the side, appraising Anna as if she were a fascinating painting on display at a museum.

Anna felt small underneath the woman's gaze. Smaller and weaker than she had ever felt in her life.

Anna stepped back, and the woman laughed, the same high, piercing cackle that Anna had heard in the forest.

"Do I frighten you, little hunter?" asked the woman. She crossed her legs and grinned, revealing perfectly straight, white teeth. "I'm sorry if my forest was a bit rough bringing you here, but it does truly hate people who threaten my well-being."

"You—you're the Watcher?" Anna stuttered.

"I go by many names," the woman answered. "The Bell Witch. The Witch of Callan Road." She turned her head to the other side, still studying Anna with an artistic precision. "I believe humans in this part of the country call me the Watcher."

Anna's breath hitched.

Anna had done it. She'd found *her*. She'd found the witch who had cursed the family and evaded the

Grimsbane hunters for hundreds of years—the witch who ensured every male relative Anna had either had died or was going to die a horrible, miserable death.

Anna had found the Watcher, but she was unarmed and alone, trapped with someone who had proven herself capable of murder centuries ago.

Anna's gaze found a deer skull beside a table leg, smiling crookedly despite its macabre state.

"You . . ." Anna gulped, glancing at the jar of eyes. Her voice sounded remarkably small. "You eat people?"

The Watcher chuckled darkly and stood up, placing her hands on the table and leaning forward. Her fingers spread out like great, white spiders upon its wooden surface.

"Spoken like a true hunter," the Watcher mused, sneering. "I don't eat people, though people like you certainly love to spread that rumor."

At the mention of people like her, Anna's brain snapped back into place. There was a reason she was here. "My brother—"

The Watcher nodded, elegantly moving around the table toward Anna. Her footsteps made no noise as she crossed the creaky floor. "The first human to realize that I use Hot Foot Powder to avoid witch hunters—a very clever boy."

Anna was about to take another step back, but she hesitated. The Watcher slowly inched toward her, her eyes gleaming with a haughty, mischievous excitement. Anna had never been this afraid in her life, but she had to be brave for Billy.

Anna hardened her resolve and stood up straighter, trying to look powerful. "Where is he?"

The Watcher smiled as if she'd been waiting for Anna to ask. She raised a hand and snapped her fingers.

A thud shook the floor and Anna spun around.

Billy lay upon the floor beside the hearth, but he didn't look at all like himself. He had a purple bruise on his chin and a black eye. His clothing was torn and dirty, his feet were bare and muddy, and he had a thin layer of sweat on his brow. Billy shivered violently. His eyes flicked back and forth under closed eyelids, almost like he was having a nightmare.

"Billy!" screamed Anna, falling to her knees next to her brother. She grabbed his shoulders and shook them. His head lolled uselessly from side to side. "C'mon, Billy! Wake up! Please, wake up!"

"It's no use," said the Watcher plainly. "He's—"

"WHAT DID YOU DO TO HIM?" shouted Anna, rounding on the witch.

The Watcher raised her hand. Suddenly Anna's tongue latched to the roof of her mouth, squeezing against it as if held there by a painfully tight clamp.

The Watcher pointed at her. "The next time you speak out of turn, I will cut out your tongue and make you swallow it. Do you understand?"

Anna nodded quickly.

The Watcher put her hand down, and Anna gasped.

"Good," said the Watcher daintily before continuing. "Your brother is simply getting what's coming to him. Trapped in an illusion of my own making. Should last a few hours before the memory erasure begins."

"Memory erasure?" asked Anna, her voice leagues above its usual pitch as she stared in horror at her brother.

The Watcher nodded, as if pleased with her handiwork. "A simple charm. Sure, it'll leave him comatose for a few weeks, maybe a few months, but I can't have him go blabbering to your family about Hot Foot Powder, can I? Not when it's the only thing that's kept me safe all these years."

"He didn't do anything wrong, though!" shouted Anna, placing a protective arm over Billy. "He didn't do anything! He was just trying to break the curse—"

"A curse rightfully bestowed upon your family."

"But Billy didn't do anything to *deserve* a curse! It's not his fault!"

"Stupid little thing, aren't you?" The Watcher examined Anna with distaste, clicking her tongue disapprovingly. "Disgusting, really, how much you resemble Diligence."

Anna's mind flashed to the diary lying at the bottom of her backpack. She felt a fire light in her stomach, a fire that sparked with the faces of all the women who had inspired her throughout her life.

"I'm *proud* I resemble Diligence!" Anna shouted, sitting up taller and scrunching her nose. "Diligence Grimsbane is the greatest witch hunter of all time!"

The Watcher snarled. "Foolish girl! Proud of a past you don't understand!"

"I understand it perfectly!" yelled Anna. "We didn't do anything wrong!"

"Nothing *wrong*?" The Watcher cackled again. Her joyful screams pierced the night as she continued to glide forward. "Spoken like a typical Grimsbane! Speaking of Grimsbanes," said the Watcher, finally reaching Anna. "I can't have you telling your family about my secret either."

A delicate white teacup full of a steaming black liquid appeared in the witch's hand.

She extended the cup to Anna. "Drink up, little hunter."

Anna glanced quickly at the Watcher, who was staring at her with a silent, frenzied delight. Anna's gaze found Billy, still trapped under the witch's memory spell.

Had Billy drunk the potion?

Anna shook her head. "No way."

"Oh, don't worry," said the Watcher, taking another step forward. "I made this one especially for you."

Anna pressed her lips shut and shook her head.

The Watcher's lamplike eyes narrowed.

For a moment, Anna feared the Watcher was going to turn her into a toad. Then the witch darted forward with impossible speed. One long-fingered hand latched on to Anna's jaw, while the other precariously tipped the teacup beside her mouth, the steaming liquid threatening to spill out at any second.

"Open—your—mouth," the Watcher growled through gritted teeth.

Anna wrenched her head from side to side, trying to shake out of the witch's hold.

The Watcher grasped Anna's jaw tighter, pulling downward with such strength it felt like someone had tied a school bus to Anna's cheekbones. "Open—your—mouth—Grimsbane."

Anna twisted desperately, staring in horror at the black liquid sludging like thickened oil in the teacup.

The Watcher snarled. She grabbed Anna's neck and dragged her upward. With one arm, she slammed Anna against the wall.

Anna's head ricocheted off the splintery wood, and she gasped in pain.

The Watcher forced her jaw open and slid the potion down her throat.

Anna gagged and stumbled, nearly falling forward as the witch dropped her. Her throat burned as if she'd swallowed a hot poker. Her windpipe tightened like a rag being wrung out. She clutched her neck.

Spots darted across her vision as she slipped to the floor. Anna landed beside Billy, turning to face her brother as the world began to fade away.

She felt something grab her chin and looked up to see the Watcher leaning over her, her thick, silvery hair falling into Anna's face.

"Are you ready, little hunter?"

The room began to spin like a carousel, faster and faster and faster until everything was a blur but Anna and the witch.

The Watcher began to transform. Her silvery hair shot back into her head, growing shorter and thinner until there was practically no hair left. Her smooth, ivory skin became marred, peppered by wrinkles, age spots, and knots. Her straight, pearly teeth shifted—yellowing, sinking, and rising until they looked like gravestones sticking out of her gums. All that remained the same were her eyes—a haunting, vivid yellow.

Anna tried to turn her head away, but the Watcher's grip was too strong.

"Are you ready to face the truth, little hunter?"

Anna's feet hit grassy ground and she stumbled, falling to her knees.

The burning sensation in her throat was gone, but that was the least of her worries.

She staggered to her feet and turned in circles, taking in the scene surrounding her—the thunder echoing above the village, the freezing wind and rain soaking her hair, the sound of waves crashing against the cliffs a thousand feet below, the salty spray of sea air on her face.

Where *was* she?

21

The First Hunter

Anna looked about the landscape, doing her very best to get her bearings. She was standing on the edge of a precipice overlooking a churning black sea. Lightning flashed, and Anna jumped, turning away from the cliff. She was just beside a small village composed of stone cottages that sat upon the ground like squat old men around a table. Despite the late hour and the storm, the village was teeming with life.

"To the cliff!" she heard one man scream.

"The pitchforks!" yelled another.

"Hold her!" shouted a third. "Do not let her escape!"

A mass of hard-faced men stumbled up the hill to the cliff, marching purposefully through the wind and rain, cheering as they brandished pitchforks, axes, and guns high over their heads. Two men toward the front held a struggling woman by the arms. The only calm person in the whole bunch marched at the front of the crowd—a tall, imposing figure with an impressive mustache that he twirled with one long pointer finger.

The mob reached the crest, and Anna moved to avoid them, certain they were going to yell at her, but they didn't so much as look at her. They simply continued with their business, seemingly oblivious to her presence. The villagers jeered at the trapped woman, circling her like a frenzy of hungry sharks.

The imposing man held up a hand, and the crowd fell silent.

"What evidence does the village present?" asked the man in a booming baritone as loud as the thunder, ignoring the tumultuous storm that whipped at his thick wool cloak.

"She owns a broomstick!" exclaimed a villager.

"She sings!" shouted another.

"I have heard her as well! She sings!"

"A mole upon her face! The true mark of a witch!"

"Mercy Matthews," said the man, staring at the woman with cold, uncaring eyes, "you stand accused of witchcraft. How do you answer?"

"I did not!" screamed the woman. "I swear I—"

The crowd jeered at her again, erupting into shouts.

The man held up a hand, and the crowd once again quieted, seeming to bow under the very weight of his being. He slowly stepped forward, approaching the struggling woman with the air of someone who thought the world would stop spinning if he asked it to. "It is in the opinion of the village, and of myself, that you, Mercy Matthews, are a witch. Do you wish to repent?"

"I am not a witch!" shrieked the woman.

The man stared at her for a moment, his pale eyes narrowing. The villagers gazed at him expectantly, like dogs waiting for a human to throw them a steak.

"Very well," he said coldly. He turned swiftly to the villagers holding her. "You know what to do."

"NO!" screamed the woman, thrashing and screaming like a fish caught in a net as the men carrying her started to make their way to the cliff side. "NO, PLEASE!"

"Wait!" Anna shouted, rushing forward.

The men drew the woman back and hurled her off the cliff.

Anna screamed.

The men erupted into cheers. Anna couldn't believe

what she was seeing. They'd just thrown someone off a cliff. How could they be happy about that?

"Good show, men! Good show!" exclaimed the man at the front of the crowd, shaking the hands of the villagers, letting out a cheerful laugh—the first bit of emotion that Anna had seen from him. "I believe that clears up the last of the witches in Cornwallshire!"

"Forty-eight witches gone!" exclaimed a man. "Every witch disposed of!"

Forty-eight?

Anna stared over the cliff, examining the rocks below with a sick feeling rolling through her stomach.

Forty-eight people thrown over a cliff for owning a broomstick?

The scene melted around Anna like candle wax, bubbling up and changing until it was daytime—a damp, chilly day similar to those in Witchless. Anna was on a narrow, muddy road not unlike those in the Not-So-Witchless Woods, where something very important seemed to be happening.

The imposing man strode purposefully away from the village, clutching a leather bag and wearing a thick, black traveling cloak with a tall hat that made him look like a Pilgrim. The villagers hurried after him like a swarm of bees following their queen.

Anna's sneakers sloshed desperately against the ground as she struggled to catch up with the scene playing in front of her.

"Reverend, you must stay!" shouted one of the men, slipping in the mud. "What if another witch enters the village?"

The imposing man stopped and turned, his mustache bristling as he gazed upon the hard-faced men following him. "I have done my duty as a reverend. I have disposed of all witches in Cornwallshire, and as there are no women left, it seems unlikely that any witches should spring up after my departure to the New World."

Anna turned to the men of the village, who looked positively distraught at the thought of the reverend leaving them.

The reverend sighed. "There is no purpose for me here anymore, men. It is high time I retired. I am thirty-four. I have lived a long, full life. Now all I want is a place where there are no witches or people to bother me."

The villagers stared at him in silence.

The man tipped his hat at them and continued down the road, not sparing even a backward glance to the citizens of Cornwallshire, now without their wives, without their daughters, and without their reverend.

"Shame, really," said a man, finally breaking the silence. "Reverend Perseverance was the best witch hunter we ever had."

Before Anna could process what she'd heard, she felt the ground tilt under her and throw her to the side.

She landed harshly on a dusty path and winced as her ribs groaned in pain. She stood up, brushed herself off, and looked around.

Anna was in the Not-So-Witchless Woods on a hot, gray summer day, and she wasn't alone. Reverend Perseverance knelt by the "Witchless, New Cornwallshire" sign, accompanied by a woman whose face was mostly obscured by a bonnet.

Reverend Perseverance leaned back and stared at the sign a moment, before chuckling quietly to himself. "Alone at last."

This was not at all how Anna pictured the famous Reverend Perseverance Grimsbane. She always imagined him more like Dad and Billy—nice and fun and full of light. She hadn't imagined him to be a hermit, and certainly hadn't expected him to be a witch hunter.

Or a murderer.

Anna moved around the sign to get a better look at the woman and gasped.

For a moment, Anna thought the woman was Madeline, but she soon realized that wasn't the case. The woman's nose was longer, and her jaw was a bit narrower. Plus, she had significantly less muscle and makeup than Anna's older sister. This woman seemed far more serious as well, scowling at the sign as she whittled away at it, narrowing her dark eyes in concentration.

"There," she finally said, standing up and brushing off her skirt. "Population: two."

Reverend Perseverance nodded, turning to the woman. "Would you like to see the cottage, Diligence?"

The woman nodded. "As of today, it is our home. I see no reason to wait."

With that, Perseverance and Diligence set off into the forest, his hand sliding into hers.

Anna scoffed.

That was Diligence Grimsbane?

That was the most famous witch hunter in her family?

The woman was so remarkably unremarkable it was almost impossible to envision her taking on the most dangerous witches in the region throughout her lifetime, let alone being a founding member of the Knights of Van Tassel.

The forest melted away again, and Anna fell through the air, landing harshly on a smooth, wooden floor.

"Jeez," Anna muttered, rubbing her shoulder as she sat up and looked around.

She was inside a quaint cabin bedroom, where two people were sleeping softly on a simple wooden bed. Anna could barely hear their deep breathing over the rain buffeting the cabin walls.

Just as Anna stood up, an earsplitting bang echoed outside.

Anna shouted in surprise.

Reverend Perseverance shot up in bed, peering into the piercing darkness that surrounded him.

Anna heard a rustle—a voice, barely above a whisper, only slightly stifled by the cabin walls and the rain.

Something was moving outside the cabin.

"Diligence." Reverend Perseverance tried to shake his wife awake. "Diligence, did you hear that?"

Diligence turned over.

"DILIGENCE!"

Diligence sprang from the bed as if she'd sat on a tack. "What?" she shouted, pulling a shawl around her shoulders, moving to grab her shoes. "Is it the neighbors? Should I wake the children?"

"There is no one for miles," he reminded her.

Diligence seemed to remember this, wilting slightly as she realized she had gotten out of bed for nothing. Anna noticed Diligence was a bit bigger than when she'd seen her last—particularly around her middle. She was so pregnant, it looked like she was carrying a beach ball under her nightgown.

A high, penetrating cackle rang through the night like a bell in a church steeple. Reverend Perseverance locked eyes with Diligence, and the two of them crept past Anna to the window. In their white nightclothes, they looked like slightly yellowed ghosts in need of ironing.

It was upon looking out the window that Anna discovered that Witchless, New Cornwallshire, was no longer witchless.

A woman wearing a dark dress and cloak stood in the clearing beside a cauldron, completely oblivious to the man and woman watching her from the window. She stirred the cauldron with a long stick. It began glowing, releasing a thick, red smoke that hung upon the clearing like a shroud.

Reverend Perseverance scoffed. Anna jumped and faced him.

"*Witches,*" he growled, twisting his mustache with a pronounced scowl. "What a nuisance. Up to no good, she is. Wait here."

Diligence nodded.

Reverend Perseverance grabbed his rifle off the wall and marched outside. He slumped toward the witch, his bare feet sinking into the mud, rain soaking his pajamas. Anna followed closely behind.

The witch didn't notice him.

Reverend Perseverance raised his gun.

"Pardon me!" he shouted.

The witch continued stirring the cauldron.

"Pardon me!"

The witch continued stirring the cauldron.

"PARDON ME!"

The witch looked up. Anna's stomach sank to her knees.

The Watcher stood before her in a younger form. Though her unblinking eyes remained the same and her skin was as glowing as ever, her hair wasn't silver, but rather a thick, chestnut mane that fell halfway down her back. The Watcher examined Perseverance, clearly more annoyed than anything.

"Witch!" shouted Reverend Perseverance, drawing himself to his full height with as much dignity as he could muster in his nightclothes. "My name is Reverend Perseverance Grimsbane, and I am here to inform you that this is Witchless, New Cornwallshire—population of four! Not only are you trespassing on private land, but you are also a *witch*! As a reverend, I will be forced to shoot you if you do not immediately repent and vacate the premises!"

"Repent?" asked the Watcher, continuing to stir. "Interesting suggestion, but I have no intention of doing that. I only came here to deliver a message. I suggest you go back inside, Reverend—that you gather your family, lock your doors, and do not open the windows until morning. This is All Hallows' Eve, and there are creatures about the forest, drawn here by my power. They won't be here long, but the evening will end poorly for you if you don't take the necessary precautions."

"I will not repeat myself again!" shouted Reverend Perseverance. His hands tightened around his rifle. "Repent and vacate the premises immediately, or I will shoot!"

She ignored him.

Anna noticed Diligence crack the cabin door,

still remaining inside, her hand cradling her bulging stomach.

Reverend Perseverance cocked his gun.

The Watcher's gaze snapped up at him, her yellow eyes reflecting the shimmering, red liquid lighting the cauldron.

The Watcher sighed. "Reverend, I suggest you leave me alone. I'll gladly do the s—"

BANG!

The Watcher raised her right hand, and time froze.

The bullet remained suspended less than a foot away from the gun. The bubbling cauldron stopped bubbling, and the rain stopped falling. Diligence stood frozen in the doorway. All that moved were Anna, the Watcher, and Diligence's and Reverend Perseverance's eyes, growing wide with terror as the witch stalked toward Perseverance, who remained frozen in place.

"I told you to leave me alone, and you did not listen." She stopped just in front of Reverend Perseverance, a smirk playing at the corner of her mouth. "You will pay dearly for that, Perseverance Grimsbane."

The wind began to howl furiously, ripping twigs and leaves and branches off the trees surrounding Reverend Perseverance. The darkness in the Watcher's eyes leaked past the whites, stretching until her eyes were indistinguishable from black marbles.

"I know all about you, Perseverance," the Watcher stated. "I know about your history as a witch hunter, how you celebrated after murdering innocent people—how you laughed when condemning them to death."

It was then that the trees began to sing—the same hollow voices singing the song Anna had heard a thousand times tonight, about laughing at someone's death, and being the next one to die.

> *Don't you laugh when the hearse*
> *goes by*
> *'Cause you might be the next to die.*
> *They'll wrap you up in a clean*
> *white sheet*
> *And put you down about six*
> *feet deep.*

Anna remembered something that Taileybones had said earlier this evening—back when they first met. He thought the older trees were singing to recount their memories. Anna now knew what they were singing about. The trees were recounting The Watcher's memories of Perseverance's celebration of the murder of the forty-eight women in Cornwallshire, and warning Perseverance of what would happen next.

Anna watched as Reverend Perseverance tried with all of his might to move, straining with every fiber of his being to lift even a finger, but it was no use. He was stuck in place.

The Watcher smiled and began to speak, her voice echoing as if spoken by a hundred women at once, loud enough to be heard for miles.

"For the murder you tried to commit tonight and the murders you have committed throughout your life, all of your male descendants and every man who joins your family will be cursed. They will die suddenly and unusually, before their time, just like the women you have murdered."

The Watcher slowly raised the index finger on her left hand.

Anna watched in horror as the bullet turned. As if it were swimming through molasses, the bullet moved sluggishly toward Reverend Perseverance's chest, growing closer and closer as the witch grinned.

"The curse cannot be undone until your descendants repent for your actions."

The bullet touched his chest.

The wind stopped.

Reverend Perseverance's eyes darted between the

witch and the bullet. His heart beat noisily against his rib cage, as if desperate to escape its doomed fate.

"I wonder if you have a heart for the bullet to go through," mused the Watcher.

She slammed her hand to her side.

The rain began to fall. The witch, cauldron, and smoke disappeared.

Reverend Perseverance fell like a rag doll dropped by a child.

The cabin door swung open with a bang, and Anna jumped. Diligence ran into the clearing. She fell to her knees beside Reverend Perseverance's corpse, weeping as she clutched her husband's body.

No!" screamed Diligence, holding his head in her hands. "No! Please, no!"

Diligence laid her head on Reverend Perseverance's bloodied chest. She let out a horrible sob, and Anna's heart wrenched.

Reverend Perseverance, of course, didn't respond. He just continued to stare emptily into the night, his pale eyes reflecting the moon and stars shining down upon the clearing. His gaze was wide and fearful— eternally frozen in his last, terrifying moment.

Diligence let go of him. Tears continued to stream down her face, half of which was now covered in her husband's blood. She put her hand to her bulging stomach and sighed shakily, breathing deeply through her nose.

Two small girls in nightclothes emerged from the doorway, rubbing sleep out of their eyes, woken up by the ruckus.

"Mother?" one of them called.

Diligence turned. A fierce light appeared in her eyes as she stared at her daughters, a distinct combination of hatred, fury, and grief hardening her gaze as she slowly turned from the children to the clearing. She stared at the spot where the Watcher had stood just a second before—the spot where the witch had killed her husband and cursed her unborn son.

Diligence Grimsbane wiped her eyes and picked up her husband's discarded gun.

In a flash of light, Diligence disappeared.

Anna blinked in confusion. She looked about, but the clearing was completely empty. Even the cabin was gone.

"Not what you expected, little hunter?" crooned the Watcher's voice, reverberating around her as if spoken from every direction.

Anna didn't know how to respond. She thought she knew the story of Reverend Perseverance. She never expected him to be a murderer. She hadn't expected him to fire the bullet that killed him. The Watcher had been trying to warn the Grimsbanes about the cryptids in the forest. She'd told them to lock their doors and stay out of trouble. The Watcher had been trying to keep them safe, and Perseverance had tried to shoot her.

"Don't want to play my game, do you?" asked the Watcher, the boredom evident in her voice. "Perhaps you'd enjoy something a bit more exciting, then."

The scene around Anna dissolved like paint in water. Trees and grass and dirt vanished as the world swirled into darkness. Anna felt a tremendous pressure and clenched her eyes shut, waiting for a weightless drop into nothingness.

No drop came.

Anna slowly opened her eyes.

She was standing at the end of a familiar driveway lined with long, overgrown grass, hearses, and motorcycles. A porch wrapped in pool noodles and cheerleading mats stood before her. Beyond that was a wide-open door, a house full of lights, and the promise of safety.

Anna was back at the Grimsbane Family Funeral Home.

22

The Hunted

Anna resisted the powerful urge to run straight into the house and find Mom and Dad.

She studied the funeral home cautiously, the familiarity of it threatening to bring down her defenses. A rainlike smell drifted on the cool, fall breeze. It looked *just* like her house, but the Watcher couldn't have transported her home, right?

Anna inched slowly up the driveway. The overgrown grass brushed against her ankles. She could hear laughter ring out from the open door. Her heart ached, urging her to move faster.

"What's taking so long, little hunter?" asked the

Watcher in her reverberating tone. "Don't you want to see your family?"

Anna reached the front porch and grabbed on to the pool-noodle railing, tracing the foam with her fingers. The door was open, but there was no one standing in the foyer.

Every light in the house was on. Someone just had to be in there.

Anna carefully walked up the stairs and crossed the porch. The rubbery cover of the cheerleading mats squeaked against the soles of her muddy shoes.

Anna stepped into the foyer.

The lights dimmed to their lowest setting.

The door slammed shut behind her.

Anna pulled at the doorknob. Locked. She slid to the front window to see if there was anything outside, but it was completely black, as if the outside had ceased to exist the moment she stepped inside.

Anna turned around and froze.

Diligence Grimsbane stood shrouded in the light emanating from the open basement doorway, which barely illuminated the family crest above the door: two axes crossed over each other, with "Engage. Incapacitate. Kill." written underneath it. Diligence peered into the foyer with a cold gaze, her eyes wrinkling around the corners. Now she sported men's clothing, streaked silver hair, and a more muscular physique than Madeline. Diligence plodded into the room, closely followed by two teenage girls who looked remarkably like her. All three held rifles, wore knives strapped across their chests, and had two axes on their backs.

"Careful," warned Diligence, falling to one knee and preparing to aim her rifle. "It should be close by. Remember the rules?"

"Engage, incapacitate, kill," recited the girls in unison.

Diligence nodded in approval, pointing her gun at the front door.

Anna watched as Diligence slowly moved the gun in the direction of the stairs. Her aim inched past the window.

Diligence smirked. "Hellhounds are much easier to track than witches."

Diligence aimed at Anna and shot.

Anna screamed and ducked. She waited for a moment, shaking from head to foot, the image of a rifle pointed directly at her permanently melded to her brain. It was a vision of the past, Anna knew. It had to be a vision of the past. It was a trick the Watcher had created to torment her.

That didn't make it seem any less real.

A slamming door pulled Anna out of her thoughts.

A miserable-looking boy in colonial clothing and a leather helmet no older than Madeline marched through the foyer. He stamped past Anna and up the stairs. The plush carpeting muffled his footfalls.

"Jonathan!" shouted a sallow-faced blond girl around Anna's age, exiting the Grand Viewing Room and running after him. "Jonathan, wait!"

When she passed, Anna noticed something familiar clutched in her hand—a leather-bound journal with writing etched into the front. Diligence's diary.

Anna stood and quickly followed them upward.

"Jonathan, are you really going to make me chase after you?" asked the girl, stomping after the boy.

The boy abruptly stopped on the second-floor landing, crossing his arms.

"Are you all right?" asked the girl.

The boy sighed, turning with a heavy expression that reminded Anna painfully of Billy. "Mother says I am not permitted to leave Witchless. She thinks the curse will kill me like it killed Father."

"You will get your chance to fight in the war," the girl said, smiling. "We have never been closer to finding the Watcher."

Jonathan seemed unconvinced, staring at her with a painfully unamused expression.

The girl studied him for a moment before holding out the diary. "Want to read about the hag Aunt Hester tomahawked in Philadelphia?"

The siblings disappeared, and Anna blinked.

A thud resounded on the floor above her, accompanied by a bloodcurdling scream that pierced her heart.

Instinct took over. Anna thundered up the stairs, skipping two at a time to see which of her relatives was hurt.

She reached the third floor and shouted in surprise.

An old woman in a petticoat stumbled down the right-side hallway, fearfully glancing behind as she clutched her forehead. Blood seeped between her fingers and dripped onto the beige carpeting. Anna automatically rushed forward to help, then froze.

A heavily armed Grimsbane woman dressed in an overcoat and pants exited a cousin's bedroom. The Grimsbane ambled casually behind the old woman, turning an axe over in her gloved hands. She walked as if she were taking a stroll in the park, whistling loudly as an invisible source of rain drenched her long, black hair.

"Y'know," the Grimsbane said, "I think I could outdo Sherman if the Union would let me fight." She sighed, turning to the old woman. "What're your thoughts on that, witch?"

The old woman staggered, nearly running into Anna, before turning back to look at the Grimsbane with black, marblelike eyes. "Please—"

The Grimsbane rolled her eyes. "At least *try* to make this a fight."

She threw the axe.

Anna turned away just as the vision dissipated.

Anna took a deep breath, her thoughts clouded with anxiety and fear. She knew a vision could hop out at any moment, from behind any of the doors lining the hallway. Just a few hours ago, she would have been so excited to see her family's history up close. Now, seeing it from all perspectives, she thought it was absolutely horrifying.

Anna heard a noise like a bouncing ball and turned.

A single, black-heeled shoe bounded down the staircase. It skipped two or three stairs at a time, as if someone had kicked it off. It landed on the floor just in front of Anna. She leaned over and examined it.

There was blood on the heel.

Anna clutched the shoe in her hand as she marched

slowly up the stairs, a strange mix of curiosity and dread filling her. She didn't want to see whatever was at the top, but she couldn't help it. She just had to know.

Anna reached the fourth floor.

"Y'know women can vote now?" A Grimsbane woman dressed like a mobster circled a black-eyed flapper, bound and gagged in the middle of a salt circle just in front of the stairs. Lines of mascara traced down the woman's face as she struggled, tears rolling readily down her cheeks. She was missing her left shoe.

Anna watched as a second Grimsbane girl stepped out of the left-side hallway, pulled out a lighter, and lit a cigarette. "There are better things to do with one's time than witchcraft."

"Solid point, Dotty," said the first Grimsbane as she puffed on her own cigarette. "Why didn't you take up politics, witch?"

The flapper said something through her gag, glaring at the Grimsbanes with the utmost hatred.

"No answer?" asked Dotty, raising an eyebrow. "You know what that means, Minnie?"

Minnie nodded, playfully holding up the lighter she'd used to light her cigarette just seconds before.

She threw the lighter at the witch.

"NO!" Anna screamed, rushing forward to catch it.

The scene froze, contracted, and dissolved like a sandcastle in the wind.

It was then that the sound of a page turning began to echo through the vision. It was impossibly loud, as if someone were turning the largest book ever written. The noise was clearly coming from the attic. The noise picked up—gaining speed until it sounded like someone was riffling through the pages, turning them as fast as they possibly could.

Anna paused. Worry built in her stomach as she stared at the staircase leading to the attic. What was she going to find up there?

"Best get a move on, little hunter," crooned the Watcher, her voice overpowering the music. "Don't want me to get *bored*."

Anna took a deep breath and calmly, carefully, began her trek upward. The sound grew ever louder as she scaled the staircase. Even though the thick carpeting and plush surfaces normally muffled this sort of thing at home, the page-turning sound overwhelmed her every sense, sharply juxtaposing the aching dread growing in her chest.

When she reached the landing, Anna paused.

All of the lights were out but the one in Anna's bedroom. Her door opened and closed on its own accord, swinging like a barn door in a tornado.

The page turning slowed down, lurching forward in a deep and mechanical fashion, like a great machine stopping. It reached the original sound again—a single page being turned over and over and over again. The light began to flicker.

Anna took a step forward, then another, then another, silently willing herself to remain on her feet as her heart thudded in her chest. She knew it was a vision, but something about it being her own room made Anna's blood freeze.

For her, the attic had always been the safest part of the house—the one place where no one made fun of her or called her stupid or told her she was too little to do things. This was her place, and now it wasn't safe.

Anna reached her bedroom and stepped into the flickering light.

The page turning stopped.

The light steadied.

Anna was in her parents' office.

* * *

Anna turned about in confusion, wondering how that was possible, until she heard the Watcher laugh.

"Had enough of other people's history?" asked the Watcher. "Want to get a taste of your own?"

"Why would you hunt a *necromancer* on Halloween?"

Anna turned and saw her mother sitting in the leather armchair across from her father's desk. Anna saw herself from earlier, still dressed in her undead-skater costume, staring attentively at Mom, desperately hanging on to every word she yelled into the telephone.

"Well, I'm sorry, Tom, but I'm not sending my relatives into a death trap just because you and your family were stupid enough to engage—" Mom held the phone away from her ear as the man on the other end began shouting, exchanging an eye roll with Past Anna as she took the coffee. "Thanks."

"Who's that?" Anna watched herself ask her mother.

Mom once again put her phone on mute. "Tom Jackson, head of Ohio's branch of the Knights of Van Tassel. Seems he and some of his kids decided to take on a witch last night. They're finishing the job in a few hours and want me to send some people down to help."

Past Anna furrowed her brow. "Why wouldn't you?"

"Number one rule of hunting: engage, incapacitate, and kill."

The words reverberated throughout the vision as if spoken in an empty warehouse. Time slowed as Anna realized where that advice, that *rule*, had come from. What that rule that defined her family's actions for generations meant.

Don't negotiate. Don't question. Just kill the witch as soon as you find them.

"Number two rule of hunting: never, ever hunt on Halloween," explained Mom. "Like I said during the family meeting, on Halloween any area around a witch turns into a cryptid soup."

"Gross," said Past Anna.

"Exactly. No one likes fighting cryptid soup." Mom scrunched her face at the shouting on the other end of the phone. "Except Tom, apparently."

Past Anna laughed.

The scene froze.

Anna crossed the room to examine her past self. It was a strange feeling, seeing one's own face lit up with laughter, especially when one realized the joke their past self was laughing at wasn't funny at all. She thought back to Perseverance Grimsbane laughing after the men of Cornwallshire had hurled a woman off a cliff. She remembered the trees' song, about laughing at death, not realizing it was coming for you next.

Why hadn't Anna thought to question what Mom said? Why had she *laughed* at what Mom said?

The Grimsbane women didn't just hunt witches and cryptids. They killed people without questioning whether or not they were actually evil, without hearing their side of the story. They sided with whoever reported the witch every time, killing without question.

Anna thought back to Rosario, to all the great memories she had with her, and to all the hurtful things she'd said tonight.

Why had she said those things? Why hadn't she questioned her family? Did she ever once stop to question whether witch hunting was *right*?

Anna realized it was getting harder to draw breath. The vision seemed to be constricting around her, melting and shifting like an oil painting come to life. The specters of Mom, Dad, and herself disappeared.

The room straightened, and Anna took a deep breath, grateful to be out of the suffocating scene.

Anna looked up and recoiled.

She was in the funeral home's Grand Viewing Room.

Anna stood before a coffin, looking out at a crowd of Grimsbane women—the last three hundred forty years of Grimsbane women. She recognized the Revolutionary War girl, seated proudly beside Mom and Madeline. Great-Grandma Lenore was beside the aspiring Union soldier, and Cousin Camille sat sandwiched between Dotty and Minnie. Diligence sat in the very front row, looking as hard and stoic as ever, examining Anna with her dark eyes.

The women stared expectantly at Anna, like ghosts at an abandoned theater waiting for a performance.

Anna glanced at the coffin and stumbled back.

Reverend Perseverance's corpse was on display. His unnaturally pale eyes were wide open, staring in frozen, eternal horror at the witch who had cursed him. He still wore his bloodied pajamas, a dime-sized hole marking where the bullet he'd fired had entered his body.

Anna turned back around and screamed.

The Grimsbane women surrounded Anna, smiling grotesquely as they huddled uncomfortably close, trapping her in.

In one swift movement, like puppets controlled

by a puppeteer, the women raised their arms.

Their hands were completely covered in blood, dripping down their arms and onto the carpeted floor. Anna instinctively backed up, pressing harder against the casket.

She looked back down at Reverend Perseverance's cold, unstaring eyes as the women drew closer, their hands outstretched like zombies.

"Having fun?" The Watcher's voice echoed throughout the vision. "Still proud to be a witch hunter? Still proud to be a Grimsbane?"

Anna thought back to all her family had done in the name of breaking the curse.

The women pressed closer.

The only reason the curse had happened was because Reverend Perseverance had shot first.

A hand reached out and touched her arm.

Reverend Perseverance shot first, so the Watcher cursed them. Every Grimsbane death caused by the curse was *actually* caused by Reverend Perseverance's actions, and the Grimsbanes' failure to repent for them. It could've been broken ages ago, if they'd only realized that what they were doing—what they'd *been* doing—for hundreds of years was *wrong*.

The colonial girl ran a bloody hand through Anna's hair.

The women grew closer, grasping at Anna as she pushed out with all her might.

The Watcher said the potion was going to erase the last few hours of Anna's memory. Would it erase everything she had learned? Anna had to figure out a way to ensure everything she'd discovered about witches, ghosts, and cryptids—everything about her family history—would last when her memory got wiped. She had to ensure that the lies wouldn't get retold, but how could she do it?

Anna felt her backpack slip as a woman stroked it.

An idea suddenly sparked in Anna's brain. It was a small idea, but it was the best Anna could do under the circumstances.

Anna ripped off the backpack. She fell to her knees and wrenched the zipper open.

"What are you doing, little hunter?" asked the Watcher. "Have you grown tired of your family so quickly?"

Anna fumbled through the candy wrappers, fishing out the lighter and kindling as she struggled to avoid her family's grasping hands. "I'm doing what should've been done a long time ago."

Anna removed Diligence's diary from her bag, examining its leather-bound cover with a strange mixture of revulsion and grief. This book chronicled her entire family history—every witch they hunted, every ghost they fought, every cryptid they killed, and every lie they told. It was all here. The Grimsbanes had written every bad thing they'd ever done in this diary.

She threw the book onto the floor and moved to throw the kindling on it.

Madeline trod on the diary with her thick-soled combat boot. She stepped closer, flinging the book backward into the crowd.

"C'mon, Madeline," Anna muttered under her breath. She scooped up the lighter and kindling and held them close to her chest as she shimmied between the legs of the Grimsbanes.

She felt a bloodied hand tug at her shoulder. Someone grabbed her arm and tried to yank her back. Anna gritted her teeth and pulled forward, not taking her eyes off the diary. Anna reached out for the book.

Someone grabbed her ankle, and Anna fell to her stomach. Anna turned back to see who it was.

Diligence Grimsbane crouched behind her. She looked as gray and hard-faced as the villagers of Cornwallshire, scowling at Anna disapprovingly.

"Don't you take pride in your family legacy?" Diligence asked in the Watcher's voice, tightening her grip on Anna's ankle.

Anna drew her foot back and kicked Diligence in the face.

Diligence let go with an outraged scream.

Anna scrambled forward. She grabbed the diary with one hand and threw kindling on the book with the other, dodging an outstretched hand.

Anna picked up the lighter and stared down at the mess in front of her.

It was time to rewrite the Grimsbanes' legacy.

Anna flicked the lighter and threw it onto the diary.

The paper lit.

The vision exploded in a twist of flame and heat. The floor fell out from under Anna, and she slipped into darkness, the disappointed shrieks of the Grimsbanes fading away into nothing.

23

Burned Away

Anna's eyes shot open and she snapped up, gasping in the warm air and clutching at her throat, still fiery from the potion. She was lying on the floor of the Watcher's cottage. She could still feel the cold, phantom hands of her family clutching at her skin.

Anna took a deep, shaking breath.

"Anna?" she heard a familiar voice ask.

Anna turned.

Billy sat up, staring at her with an open mouth and wide eyes. He still had sweat on his brow, the bruise on his chin had grown bigger, and they were trapped in a murderous witch's cottage.

None of that mattered, though.

Anna launched herself sideways and flung her arms around Billy, just as he flung his arms around her. Anna clung to her brother like he was the last person left in the world, and there, in the Watcher's inescapable cottage, it honestly felt like he was.

"I'm sorry," Billy said quietly, almost as if he were praying. "I'm sorry. I'm sorry. I'm so sorry. This was so stupid."

"You're a jerk," she said, in lieu of an acceptance, but Billy understood her meaning all the same. "Are you okay? The black eye—"

"Don't worry about me," he muttered. "I know how to take a punch, even one from a tree. Are *you* okay?"

"I'm all right" Anna said. She let go of him, not letting go of his shoulder.

Billy smiled weakly. "You found what I had hidden behind the bookcase, didn't you?"

Anna nodded.

He sighed deeply. "No one was supposed to find that. I felt horrible about everyone blaming you for stealing the diary, but I thought it would all be worth it if I could break the curse. I found the page on secret societies and discovered that the members of the Order of the Third Eye could disappear. I realized there had to be some connection with the Watcher's ability to disappear, though I wasn't one hundred percent sure what it was. I did some digging online and found references to a material called Hot Foot Powder. And I found out that the guy who invented Monsters and Mayhem—who some Grimsbanes theorized was a member of the Order—had made plans to travel to Witchless for Halloween. I knew they had to be doing their Grand Ritual in the forest again, just like the page from Diligence's diary described. I planned to go to the Ritual, learn more about Hot Foot Powder, and somehow use it to hunt the Watcher before midnight, but—" Billy took a shaking breath. "I never even made it to the ritual. The Watcher knew I'd discovered her secret, and the trees caught me before I got that far. I thought I could do it on my own. I thought if I could hunt the Watcher and break the curse, then everyone would realize I'm not completely helpless, but . . . we were wrong, Anna. We were wrong about *everything*."

Anna nodded, her mind turning back to Rosario, Suvi, and Taileybones—to all of the cryptids they'd met—to everyone their family had hurt over the years. The guilt was eating her alive. "I know."

Billy looked around the cottage. "How'd you get here?"

"Long story," Anna responded, not wanting to go

into details about hellhounds, White Screamers, and the Not-Deer. "I—"

Billy looked down at her wrist and grabbed it. Anna hissed in pain as Billy turned it over, examining the bright red nail marks the trees had punctured into her skin. Billy took a deep breath, before looking back at Anna. "Who did this?"

Anna winced. "The trees. Will you let go? It kind of stings."

Billy dropped her wrist. "I'm getting us out of here, Anna. Cursed or not, I promise I'll get us out."

Anna was about to respond when she felt a hand on her arm.

Something pulled her to her feet and yanked her away from Billy.

Anna turned and recoiled. The Watcher stood above her in the form Anna had first seen her in— an older woman, but not nearly as old as her ancient form. The woman's yellow eyes narrowed in confusion as she held Anna's arm.

"Did you—" She looked Anna up and down. "You *repented*?"

"Don't touch her!" screamed Billy, pulling Anna back. He shoved her behind him, standing between Anna and the witch. "This is my fault! Not hers!"

The Watcher rolled her eyes. "Don't make me regret giving you both an antidote for the memory potion. That girl just broke one of the oldest generational curses in history. I bestowed it upon someone who tried to murder me, so I think I have a right to know how it was broken."

"She—" Billy shook his head, turning to Anna. "Anna, what is she talking about?"

The Watcher held out her hand, palm up.

Anna, knowing what the Watcher wanted to see, quickly removed her backpack and slid the zipper open, fishing around before her shaking hand finally curled around what used to be a journal.

She pulled Diligence's diary out of her backpack.

Or rather, she pulled out what remained of it.

The leather cover of the journal had darkened, shrunk, and cracked, resembling a dry patch of earth in a drought. The pages inside the diary had all but vanished, having turned black and shriveled. Even now, they still seemed to be curling slightly, still withering away in the fire that Anna had started.

Anna handed the diary around Billy to the Watcher.

The Watcher turned it over in her hand. "I cursed your family for a reason. The Grimsbanes—"

"—know they were wrong," finished Anna quickly.

"We hunted without hearing both sides of the story and without attempting to compromise. When we fought, it wasn't in self-defense. We shot first, but I know we're wrong now. Just let us go. We don't have to fight."

The Watcher blinked. She turned back to the diary.

Anna felt Billy grab her hand, squeezing it as hard as he could.

"We're sorry," Billy said. "We were wrong for so long. *I* was wrong for so long. I know I can never erase what my family did, but I want to try to fix it."

"I think we can be better," Anna finished. "If you'll give us a chance."

The Watcher chuckled slightly. "The great Grimsbane family witch hunters finally admit they were wrong?" She looked back to them. "This . . . could be *very* interesting." The Watcher raised her hand. The hair on Anna's arms stood on end. She could taste metal in her mouth.

"I'll make a deal with you, Grimsbanes," said the Watcher. "If your family promises to change your ways—if you promise to protect humans, cryptids, witches, *and* ghosts from harm, to make up for the mistakes your family made in the past, and, especially, to protect my forest from those who would hurt the cryptids that reside here, I'll be sure to refrain from cursing you. Step out of line, however . . ." Her eyes glowed an even brighter shade of yellow. "I will *certainly* know."

Anna could barely hear the wind outside the cottage, the crackling of the hearth, and the beating of her own heart. The fire reflected in the Watcher's clever yellow eyes.

Anna paused. Her family had done so many awful things, but this was a chance to make it right—to create a new legacy that still allowed them to help those who needed protecting, including the witches and cryptids they'd previously hunted.

"We'll do it," said Billy.

Anna nodded in agreement. "We'll make it right."

The Watcher smiled. For a moment, Anna thought she and Billy had said something wrong. Then the Watcher snapped her fingers.

The room lurched and twisted.

Anna's feet hit the uneven forest floor. Moonlight shone down on her and Billy. He turned about, clearly just as mystified as Anna was. She looked around for the cottage they'd been in just seconds ago, but it had completely vanished. That, or they'd been transported somewhere. It was hard to tell.

Anna took a step forward and heard something crunch under her foot.

She looked down and saw the burned remains of Diligence's diary. Billy bent over and picked it up. They examined the heavily charred journal. It was amazing something so simple could have held the key to breaking the Grimsbane curse all along.

"Hey, Anna," said Billy.

"What?"

He nudged her with his shoulder. "Happy birthday."

24

The Return

"ANNA! BILLY!"

Anna pivoted to see Suvi running along the path, a smile full of braces lighting up her face. "I told them! I told them the Watcher hadn't gotten you, and they didn't listen to me!"

Rosario stumbled out of the forest, relief washing over her as she followed Suvi.

Anna's heart sank to her knees as she saw the friend she had hurt so badly. "I—"

"You're alive!" Rosario shouted, pulling Anna and Billy into a hug. "I can't believe you're alive!"

Suvi quickly jumped in. "Where have you *been* for the last two hours?"

299

Two hours? "Um . . ." Anna looked back down at the diary and stepped away from Rosario. "Rosario, I'm really so—"

"Anna saved me from the Watcher," Billy said, clapping his hand on Anna's shoulder, "and broke the curse."

"You broke the curse?" shrieked Suvi, jumping up and down excitedly. "How'd you do it?"

Anna glanced from Suvi to Rosario, guilt eating away at her like a parasite. "I—"

"JESUS!" she heard Billy scream. He stumbled backward, staring over Anna's shoulder.

"Flattering, but no," said Taileybones as he emerged from the tree line. He chuckled as he approached Anna. "Thought we lost you there for a second, Grimsbane."

"For a minute, I did too," admitted Anna.

"I'm sorry. You know this hellhound?" Billy asked, turning to Anna.

"Billy, Taileybones," said Suvi, gesturing between them. "Taileybones, Billy."

Billy pursed his lips as he looked Taileybones up and down. Taileybones's eyes narrowed. He let out a fraction of a snarl until Billy raised his hand.

"Nice to meet you," Billy said.

"Anna, I like your brother more than you," said Taileybones, plopping down between Rosario and Suvi.

As Anna looked at her friends, she felt her heart clench. Despite everything she'd said and done, they'd still gone looking for her. "You guys . . . you guys came after me?"

"Well, yeah," said Rosario. "You were an emotional wreck. Admittedly, Suvi and I were too, but once we stopped crying and realized you'd gone after the Watcher on your own—"

"—we knew you couldn't take her on by yourself," finished Taileybones. "Despite your utterly deplorable behavior, we knew we'd feel horrible if something happened to you. I followed your scent, but it went cold about a mile away from here. It was like you'd vanished."

"So how'd you track me?" Anna asked, staring at her friends in disbelief.

"There was an orb," said Suvi, dancing like a toddler who had to go to the bathroom. "We'd basically given up when this huge, freezing cold ball of blue fire appeared! It started moving, and we followed it!"

"A cold ball of *fire* led you here?" asked Billy, raising an eyebrow.

Suvi nodded.

"What was it?" Anna asked.

"It was like a ghost," said Taileybones, shaking his head in confusion, "but it wasn't a ghost. It was strange. It was—"

"—something else!" finished Suvi excitedly. "Something else that was a spirit but wasn't a ghost led us to you! Just like you and Rosario said there was after the ritual! It wasn't scary like the ghosts; it was good! It wanted us to save you!"

Anna exchanged a confused look with Billy. She'd never heard of a cryptid, witch, or ghost like the thing Suvi was describing, but it made her curious. The "spirit"—perhaps a Grimsbane ancestor, or something that had accidentally been summoned during the Grand Ritual—was dead, but it wasn't a ghost. They clearly still had a lot to learn.

Before she could ask more about it, Taileybones spoke.

"How did you manage to break the curse?"

Anna held up the charred remains of Diligence's diary. "I, uh . . ." She paused, examining the journal, her cheeks glowing with embarrassment as she recalled how she'd practically worshipped it just hours ago. "I realized the Grimsbanes were wrong and lit a family heirloom on fire."

Suvi grabbed the diary from Anna. She inspected it, flipping the blackened pages as if she were a scientist examining a lab rat. "Now that's fascinating. You know, I really should do a *Ghouligans* episode about curse breaking, after an episode about the ball of light, of course—"

"I'm really sorry," Anna blurted, staring directly at Rosario.

Rosario furrowed her brow, giving a shaky laugh. "What?"

"I'm sorry about everything," said Anna, the words now rushing out of her like a waterfall as she turned between Rosario, Suvi, and Taileybones. "I said horrible things, and I was confused about witches and cryptids and my family, and I was being stupid. I was wrong. It's really no excuse, and I get it if you don't want to be friends with me anymore. I'm going to try to make it right in any way I can, and—"

Rosario launched herself forward and wrapped Anna in a bone-crushing hug.

Anna's apology caught in her throat. She'd expected Rosario to shout at her and get angry and call her names. The last thing in the world she'd expected was a hug.

"You aren't mad?" asked Anna.

"I was, for a while," Rosario said, hugging Anna even tighter. "But you apologized. You made a mistake, and you learned from it. I knew you'd come to your senses eventually, and I know you'll work to make things right."

Anna, despite herself, wiped a tear out of her eye. "I will." She hugged Rosario back. "I promise—for real, this time."

"GROUP HUG!" screamed Suvi, practically tackling her two friends to the ground as she leapt into the hug with the force of a thousand suns. "Billy! Taileybones! Get in!"

"I'm good," said Billy, stepping backward, his bare foot squishing into a bit of mud. "I'm not much of a hugger."

Anna rolled her eyes and tugged her brother into the hug.

"Oh, okay, jeez," said Billy as Anna and Rosario wrapped their arms around him. "Guess we're hugging now."

"*Taileybones*," sang Suvi playfully, "you know you want in."

"I have paws, and I don't hug," said Taileybones, seated stoically beside the circle.

"Everyone scoot," Rosario whispered.

The group shuffled and opened so Suvi and Anna could wrap their free arms around Taileybones, or, at least, sort of around Taileybones's side.

Taileybones barked in indignation. "Oh, well, that's just—" His shadowy demeanor seemed to crumble a bit as Anna smiled at him. "This is kind of nice, actually."

"Knew you needed a hug," Suvi muttered, nudging Taileybones with her shoulder.

"Um," said Billy, awkwardly sandwiched between Anna and Rosario. "I don't want to be the jerk who breaks up a group hug, but my feet are freezing, and our parents are probably freaking out, so we may want to start heading home."

"Xander's covering for us," Anna told him as everyone dropped the hug.

"He is?" Billy's eyes widened. "Did he seem worried about me? Does he know I—" Billy coughed, blushing. "I mean, yeah, that's good. That's good we had someone covering for us."

"Xander can make pretty convincing illusions," said Rosario, "but they'll only last so long. We should really start heading back."

"I know the way," said Taileybones, beginning to walk up the path.

Suvi and Billy quickly followed.

Rosario turned to Anna. "What happened with the Watcher?"

Anna unzipped her backpack and threw the diary in. "That," she said as she zipped it shut again, "is a very long story."

By the time they arrived at the edge of forest, the sun was already starting to rise, every story from the evening had been told multiple times over, and every single piece of Halloween candy left in Anna's bag had been devoured.

From her place in the tree line, Anna could barely see the outline of the Grimsbane Family Funeral Home, standing in the distance. Every light was on, despite the early hour of the morning.

Her family was probably worried to death.

"I'm going to take the *longest* shower," Suvi said, stifling a yawn. "Full heat, no messing about. Being clean sounds wonderful."

Rosario nodded in agreement. "And asleep. Being asleep also sounds great."

Anna wholeheartedly agreed. A night spent running through the forest, nearly getting eaten by a White Screamer, and breaking a curse did have a downside. Anna was so tired, she could fall asleep standing up.

"I guess this is where we part," said Taileybones.

Anna, Billy, Suvi, and Rosario turned to him in one fluid motion.

"What do you mean?" asked Anna.

Taileybones stared down at them, heaving a sigh as he turned to face the lights and buildings of Witchless. "Civilization is no place for a hellhound."

"A lot of people say the same thing about brujas," said Rosario, shrugging. "My family seems to be getting on just fine. You could stay with us."

Taileybones snorted. "Brujas blend in a bit easier than I do. Besides, can you picture me living in a house?"

As much as Anna hated to admit it, she knew this was true. Taileybones didn't seem like much of a city dweller, though the idea of parting from him was splitting Anna's heart in half. She remembered meeting him the previous evening, the pure fear she'd felt when he leapt from the trees, and the friendship they'd managed to build over the course of the night.

"You can visit," she offered.

Taileybones nodded. "I just might, but until then, you four can howl if you need me."

Anna blinked. "Howl?"

"Like a wolf."

Anna considered this for a moment. "All right, then."

"But you can't go!" protested Suvi, stumbling forward. "I mean, can I at least organize a *Ghouligans* interview? It'd be so cool!"

Taileybones chuckled. "I think I'd prefer to stay in the shadows." He turned to the others and addressed them as a group. "It was a pleasure escorting you."

With that, Taileybones turned and walked into the forest, a dark figure gracefully dancing between the shadows, his nublike tail swinging behind him.

Billy sighed deeply, putting his hands on his hips. "Mom and Dad are going to kill us."

Epilogue

Christmas Party

It was the week before Christmas, and Witchless, Indiana, had welcomed the winter with fervor.

Per usual, the sky was completely gray, and winter's deep freeze had replaced the crisp chill of fall. Sleet and wind buffeted Anna and Billy as they sped down the sidewalk, practically sprinting past the dramatic holiday displays lighting up the storefronts. Anna did her best not to slip on the ice and spill the two drink carriers she was balancing. Anna and Billy wove between two elderly townspeople, who rolled their eyes in unison in their wake.

Anna knew that most people in Witchless found the Grimsbanes even odder than they had two months

309

ago. This was largely due to the surprising change in the male Grimsbanes' dress and demeanor. Where they were once excessively cautious, always wearing helmets and holding on to railings with both hands, they were now just as wild and risky as the women, if not more so. They had all taken up daring hobbies like skydiving and knife juggling, and the women seemed perfectly fine with this.

Not only that, but now the men *also* disappeared from Witchless for great lengths of time, also returning sporting a myriad of strange injuries.

When the twins reached the end of the Grimsbanes' driveway, Anna smiled at the new facade of the Grimsbane Family Funeral Home. Long gone were the pool noodles, cheerleading mats, and overgrown grass that protected the men in the event they fell. Now the mansion stood just as it always should have—happy and full of life and risk.

Anna and Billy made their way up the stairs. Anna threw the front door open, nearly slamming into Great-Uncle Monty.

"Oh God! Sorry!" she yelled as she rebalanced the coffees in her hand. "Yours is the one in the front."

Great-Uncle Monty was now completely unrecognizable. The old man had dyed his hair bright blue and had Madeline double-pierce his ears the first chance he got—not to mention he now sported several tattoos, one of which was just a giant curse word across his left buttock, which he'd unfortunately decided to show the family during Thanksgiving dinner.

"Ah, Anna!" he exclaimed as he took the coffee. "Just the person I was looking for! You're very good with the skateboard, right?"

Anna looked to Billy, feeling quite awkward getting undivided attention from her great-uncle. Billy shrugged.

"Uh, yeah. I'm pretty good at skateboarding," Anna answered.

Great-Uncle Monty heaved a sigh of relief. "Oh good. I was looking for someone to teach me how to do a—" He paused, then snapped his fingers. "Oh, what's it called? The trick! The olive or the Oliver—"

"An *ollie*?" Anna asked in disbelief.

"That's it!" he exclaimed, clasping his hands triumphantly. "An ollie! You'll teach me how to do it?"

Anna nodded, smiling at Great-Uncle Monty's sudden interest in her hobby. "Yeah, sure! I'd be happy to."

"Oh good! I've gotta go tell Louis and Phineas. They've been on the lookout for new things to try too."

With that, Great-Uncle Monty brushed past her in

the direction of the open basement door before sliding down the railing, humming contentedly to himself. Anna still wasn't used to not seeing the family crest above the door. The Grimsbanes had removed it from *everything*, along with the former family motto.

"I'm gonna see if Dad needs help in the kitchen," Billy told Anna, before speeding off to the back of the house.

Anna followed Great-Uncle Monty downstairs, still doing her very best not to drop the coffee and ruin the family's mood for the day, though that was now very hard to do.

At one time, the basement had served exclusively as an area to train for witch hunts. Now it was much more than that.

Grimsbanes milled about the basement, joking and jostling as they answered phones in what looked like an open office space. There were twelve mahogany desks, and Grimsbanes occupied all of them. The holes in the maroon walls where axes had been thrown astray were now plastered over. The straw dummies had been stacked against the wall, and most of the weapons were now locked up in the cabinets in the back.

"If you're looking for people who take care of

paranormal problems, our rates just can't compare!" exclaimed Uncle Jasper into his desk phone as he took his coffee from Anna. "Yeah, I know we have a non-violence policy, but do you *really* want to hire witch hunters who would start a fire for no good reason in your neighborhood?" He paused, listening to the person on the other line. "Yeah, didn't think so."

Anna continued to another desk, where Mom was having a very different conversation with her caller.

"Yes, Mr. Van Tassel, we recognize that our new approach isn't the way things are *traditionally* done, but here at Grimsbane Family Paranormal Mediators, our philosophy is all about communication and compromise," said Mom as she took her coffee, rolling her eyes dramatically at the person on the other end.

Anna smiled and began climbing up the stairs, heading to the kitchen.

"We're going to the grocery store to get some extra cranberry sauce for dinner," Cousin Camille said in the foyer as she slid her winter boots on. "Wanna come?"

Madeline sighed dramatically. She was the only Grimsbane who didn't treat Anna like a hero after she broke the curse. Now Anna was by far the coolest cousin in the house, and she had accepted the appointment with enthusiasm, much to Madeline's chagrin.

"I would, but I can't," said Anna, already heading out the door. "Suvi and Rosario are coming over early."

"To do what?" asked Madeline, eyeing her suspiciously.

"Nothing," Anna sang playfully as she continued through the house.

"Anna, to do what?" Madeline shouted again, sticking her head through the door of the Grand Viewing Room.

Anna ignored her as she continued to the kitchen on the other side of the house. Truthfully, Suvi and Rosario weren't coming to dinner early, but were rather staying late to work on the newest episode of *Ghouligans*. Ever since the episode featuring Suvi's former bully (in which he described a bone-chilling encounter with a giant black dog that spoke perfect English) aired, Suvi's viewings and followers had skyrocketed. Now she was up to two episodes per week and seriously struggling to keep up with demand, though she wasn't complaining.

Anna found Dad in the kitchen with Billy, Great-Aunt Frances, and Grandma, proudly making a Christmas feast big enough to feed an army. Ever since the curse broke, the men, who had previously been banned from the kitchen due to the plethora of hot surfaces and sharp objects, had taken to cooking like fish to water, but none more so than Dad.

"Ah, thank you, Anna," said Dad, gratefully accepting his coffee and handing her a bowl full of stuffing. "Bring this to the dining room, please."

Anna was about to grumble but then remembered it had been she who'd insisted on the neighborhood Christmas party, so she grudgingly accepted the bowl and walked it to the next room over.

Admittedly, the transition from witch hunter to paranormal mediator had not been easy for some of the Grimsbanes. It had taken some people longer to come around than others. Three hundred forty years of witch hunting were difficult to make up for overnight, but they all agreed that trying was the most important thing. As such, they had adopted nonviolence policies, talked to other witch hunters about what Anna and Billy had discovered about the Watcher, and constantly worked to rewrite their legacy—acknowledging the bad, in addition to the good.

Anna figured the next step in trying was becoming friends with witches, and, luckily for the Grimsbanes, Anna knew a whole family of brujas living just across the street. She considered them perfect guests for a Christmas party.

Double luckily, they had agreed to come.

An hour later, Anna was waiting by the front door with Billy, Madeline, and a number of other Grimsbanes who were curious about the incoming brujas.

Anna sat beside Billy on the staircase, closest to the window and on the lowest step so she could open the door when the Ortiz-Riveras arrived. Madeline, who sat on the other side of Billy, was shaking her leg up and down nervously, her arm muscles flexing as she gritted her teeth.

Anna was perfectly fine ignoring her, but Billy just *had* to check in.

"You all right?" he asked, looking his older sister up and down. "You're gonna bore a hole in the carpet if you keep shaking like that. You've known the Ortiz-Riveras for years. What's the problem?"

"I know," said Madeline stiffly, though she stopped shaking her leg. "I just—" She ran a hand through her hair. "I keep wanting to get a salt bomb, but I know I shouldn't get a salt bomb. I feel like a jerk because I'm worried there's witches coming over, even though I know they're decent people."

"They're great people," corrected Anna. "Also, they prefer to be called brujas, not witches."

The doorbell rang.

The room fell silent, and everyone turned to Anna.

Anna quickly stood up, confidently walked to the door, and flung it open.

The Ortiz-Rivera family stood before them, looking just as uncertain as most of the Grimsbanes felt. At the front of the crowd stood Ms. Ortiz and Ms. Rivera, somehow managing to look elegant and bohemian even on the cold winter night, each holding a small child on their hip. Behind them stood Rosario's older siblings. Anna couldn't miss the way Salvador flexed his muscles under his thick coat, staring down the Grimsbanes as if daring them to attack, blocking some of the younger siblings from their view.

Xander, being Xander, was the first to raise his hand in greeting. "Greetings and salutations, Grimsbanes."

Rosario leaned out from behind Salvador, sporting an ugly Christmas sweater and holding a covered basket. "Sorry we're early. We brought cookies."

For a moment, no one spoke.

It was then that Great-Grandma Lenore stepped out from among the Grimsbanes.

They parted like the Red Sea as she approached the Ortiz-Riveras.

Anna's heart clenched. Though Great-Grandma Lenore had been among the most willing of the Grimsbanes to accept their new way of life after Anna broke the curse, she had also hunted witches for a solid sixty years. The prejudices that had fueled a lifetime of harmful actions were not easily buried or forgotten.

And so Anna watched, not breathing, as Great-Grandma Lenore approached her friend's family, knowing her reaction to the Ortiz-Riveras would define the rest of the Grimsbanes' behavior toward them.

Great-Grandma Lenore stopped at the doorway and sighed, grabbing Anna's arm for support. Madeline quickly stood to help.

"I would like to apologize for any harm my family has caused your family or those you love," said Great-Grandma Lenore, her voice croaking with age. "We have realized the error of our ways. We hope, one day, that we can earn your forgiveness."

Anna exchanged a shocked look with Billy. It was very rare for Great-Grandma Lenore to admit she was wrong, let alone ask for forgiveness in front of a crowd of Grimsbanes.

Ms. Ortiz turned to Ms. Rivera and engaged in a silent conversation. Ms. Ortiz raised an eyebrow. Ms. Rivera shrugged. Salvador shook his head. Xander gave two thumbs-ups. Ms. Ortiz shot him a look. Rosario gave them a nod toward the door, and Ms. Rivera turned back to Great-Grandma Lenore.

"We appreciate it," said Ms. Rivera.

Great-Grandma Lenore nodded and let go of Anna and Madeline, stretching her hand out to Ms. Rivera. "Welcome to our home."

Ms. Rivera took her hand and entered the house. "Thank you."

With that, the other Ortiz-Riveras followed behind, each welcomed into the room by a Grimsbane, who quickly engaged them in small talk as they made their way to the dining room.

"Dude," said Xander, slinging his arm around Billy. "We have *got* to talk about *The King of the Jewels* remake. You've seen the trailer, right?"

"Oh, uh, yeah," said Billy, blushing a bright shade of Christmas red and smiling as Xander led him out of the room. "I totally saw it." He coughed, then lowered his voice. "I liked it. Did you—did *you* like it?"

"Well, that could've gone a lot worse," said Rosario, moving to sit beside the stairs with Anna. "They all took it pretty well, though."

Anna nodded, glancing out the window. "Shame it's raining instead of snowing. Would've made for a more Christmassy Christmas party."

Rosario smirked. "Is that a magical request?"

Anna shrugged. "Your choice."

Rosario brought her hands close together, taking a deep breath as her hair started to float and her eyes turned black. She opened her hands slightly, creating an electric rippling in the air that darted directly upward and through the ceiling.

For a moment, all was quiet.

Then the fierce sleeting outside stopped. Instead, the prettiest snow that Anna had ever seen fell in its place. Bright, white snowflakes the size of marbles drifted gently from the clouds to the ground, where they stuck as if made of glue. Anna stared in wonder at the immediate change in weather and smiled, completely in awe at the magic her friend possessed.

"Should be enough for a snow day," said Rosario, smiling from ear to ear as her eyes faded back to their normal hazel state and her hair once again fell victim to gravity. "That is, if my moms don't realize it was my fault and make me change it back."

Anna nodded. She had to admit, being a paranormal mediator was cool, but something about creating your own snow day was *way* cooler.

She was glad to be friends with a lechuza.

Acknowledgments

First, I would like to thank my husband, Ben, for putting up with my decision to take the bar exam, plan our wedding, and publish my debut novel all at the same time. Thank you for your love and support throughout this process. You are amazing, and my reason for doing everything I do. I love you most ardently.

Second, I would like to thank my parents, Tim and Suzie Reardon. Mom and Dad, thank you for ensuring I have the confidence to share my stories, for always challenging me to be the best version of myself, and for the hours we spent reading *Pippi Longstocking*, *Heidi*, and thousands of other stories that made me fall in love with books. Love you both so much!

Next, to the real life Billys: Shannon and Timmy, you are the best siblings ever. I would gladly traverse a forest full of cryptids for either of you. Shannon, I'm sorry the Not-Deer gave you nightmares. Timmy, thank you for the fan art.

I would also like to thank my new family, the Stebeltons. Greg, Joell, and Joey, thank you for welcoming me with open arms. Joell, thank you for helping me with my edits and for being my writing buddy. I am holding you to the promise of finishing your book, and I can't wait to see it published.

Grandma Kate, thank you for your extremely helpful critiques of my earliest drafts and for always supporting my love of reading and writing. Grandpa Nick, thank you for encouraging me to think critically, act morally, and challenge myself in all aspects of life.

To the Reardons and Christophers, thank you for being the most amazing extended family ever, and for being cool enough as a collective to inspire the Grimsbanes.

I would like to thank the girlies, my real life Suvis and Rosarios: Sheila, Ally, Bailey, Delaney, Juliette, Bella, Grace, and Zoe. Thank you for making life so fun. Anthony, Will, and George, I am including you with the girlies.

If you taught or coached me at any point in my life, thank you for having an impact on me.

I would like to thank everyone at Jill Grinberg Literary Management, especially my fantastic agent, Larissa Melo Pienkowski, for believing in the Grimsbanes' story, for your creative ideas, and for always being in my corner. It has been such a joy working with you, and I'm looking forward to many more years of teamwork!

I would also like to thank everyone at Aladdin, including Valerie Garfield, Anna Jarzab, Heather Palisi, Olivia Ritchie, Sara Berko, and the marketing, publicity, and sales teams. I would especially like to thank my amazing editor, Anna Parsons. You have gone above and beyond to make *The Grimsbane Family Witch Hunters* the best story it can be. You have been the most wonderful champion for the Grimsbanes, and I am so thankful for everything you have done.

Jamie Green, thank you for creating the most gorgeous cover in history and for doing my characters so much justice. It makes me smile every time I look at it.

To the Flynns: Gabi, Amanda, Emily, Karen, Eliza, Laura, and Jennifer, thank you so much for our Zooms, which have kept me (mostly) sane throughout the publishing process. I am so grateful for our friendship. Yusof, thank you for being there for the highs and lows of publishing, and for kindly telling me when my ideas are awful. To Larissa's Lovelies, you are amazing agent siblings and I'm so grateful for our community!

A final thank-you to anyone reading this book. Thank you for joining Anna on her journey!